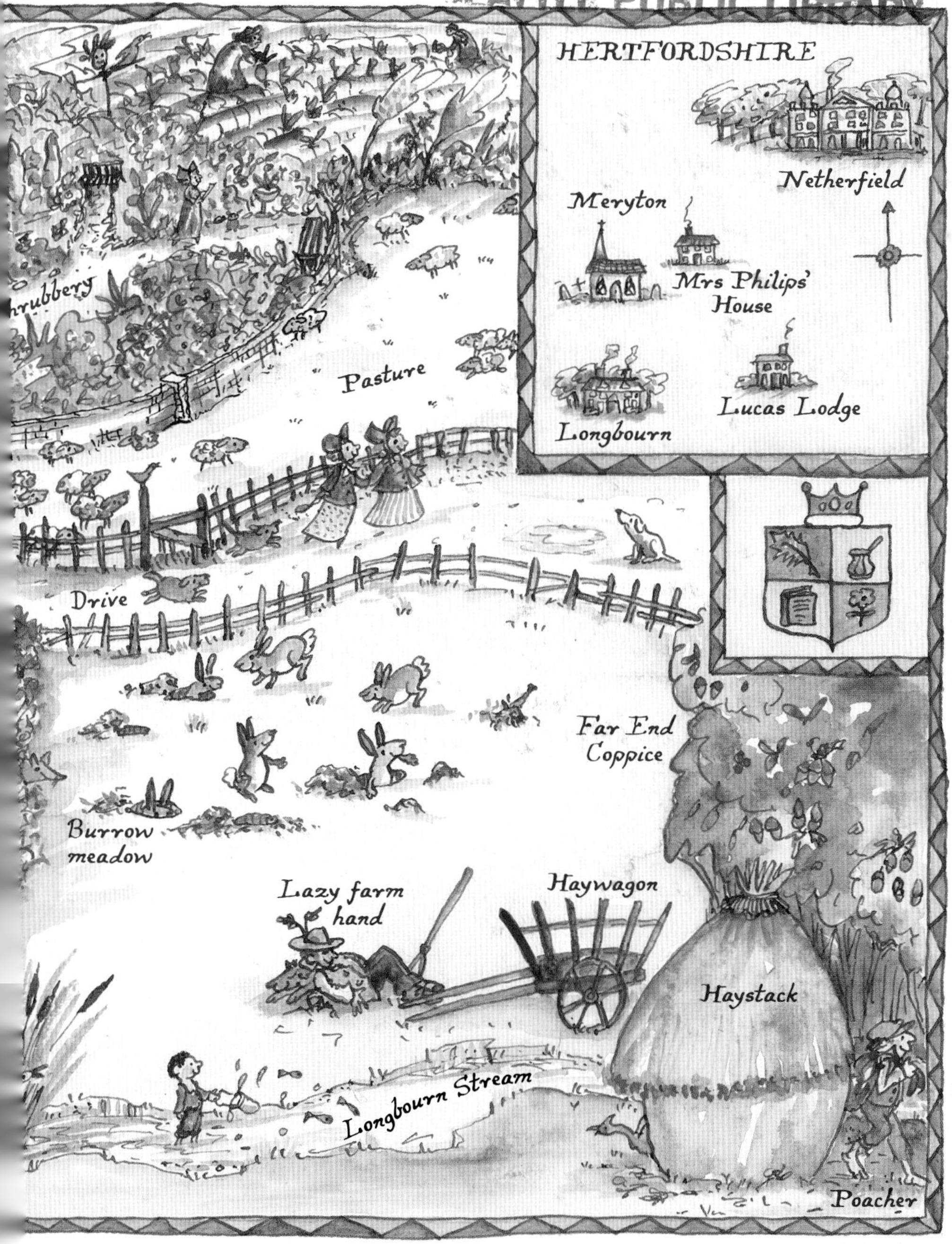
HERTFORDSHIRE
Netherfield
Meryton
Mrs Philips' House
Lucas Lodge
Longbourn
hrubbery
Pasture
Drive
Far End Coppice
Burrow meadow
Lazy farm hand
Haywagon
Haystack
Longbourn Stream
Poacher

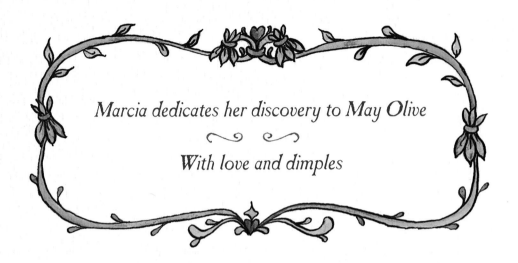

Marcia dedicates her discovery to May Olive

With love and dimples

Lizzy Bennet's Diary

1811—1812

DISCOVERED BY

MARCIA WILLIAMS

Candlewick Press

To my dear Lizzy,

As you are my only daughter with any brain, I am giving you this diary. I trust it will distract you from the idle chatter of your sisters and give you the opportunity to express your sharp observations and wit ... without distressing your mama's nerves.

Your loving papa, Mr Bennet

Christmas 1810

Mr Bennet

King George III

Mrs Bennet

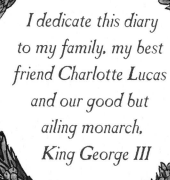

I dedicate this diary
to my family, my best
friend Charlotte Lucas
and our good but
ailing monarch,
King George III

Kitty

Lydia

Mary

Charlotte

Jane

SEPTEMBER 1811

Friday 20th

Mrs Hill keeps us all in order, even Mama.

My dear Diary,

At last I have reason to share my thoughts with you! Such excitement: our housekeeper, Mrs Hill, has just let slip that the local estate, Netherfield Park, has been let to a young, unattached gentleman! Mrs Hill's friend, who works at Netherfield, informed her that they are even now preparing the rooms.

Jane and I were helping Hill put lavender between the sheets when she told us. The news sent the lavender flying! It reminded me of confetti at a wedding. We have decided not to tell Mama about the unattached gentleman, as it is sure to send her and her nerves into a flurry of activity. The gossips of Meryton will pass on the news soon enough!

A rain-drenched Song Thrush outside my window.

Saturday 21st A VERY WET MORNING

It is most frustrating, there is no further news from Netherfield Park. No sign of the rain letting up, so I am stuck indoors listening to the idle chatter of my mother and younger sisters.

This is exactly why I had not started writing to you before. I had thought it would be better to save your pages and write a novel, for life at Longbourn is rarely disturbed by anything more than the odd domestic inconvenience. I dared hope that the arrival of a young gentleman at Netherfield might change this, but it may just be servants' tattle. I wish my dear friend Charlotte would brave the rain and pay us a call...

Lizzy's burnt the toast ... again!

A domestic inconvenience

Such news, Charlotte!

Sunday 22nd

Dearest Diary,

It is all true! Netherfield Park has been let to a Mr Charles Bingley. Mr Bingley is a young, unattached gentleman of large fortune and Mama is in raptures. She supposes that Mr Bingley must be in want of one of her five daughters for his wife! Oh, I hope so! It would be no bad thing, for should dear Papa die, Mama, my four sisters and I would be left homeless. Our home, its contents and most of Papa's income is left to a Mr Collins – a quite unknown and unloved cousin. It is a scandal that we females may not inherit. Even so, I shall never marry for money or position!

Anyway, at present, thank the good Lord, dear Papa is very much alive, for without him and dear Jane, I would surely go MAD – it is certain that my mother and younger sisters have not a sensible thought between them.

Being a man is a quite unaccountable advantage.

I suspect Mr Collins of being fat!

I am going to embroider a waistcoat for Papa; these are my buttonhole designs. Papa has a liking for strange insects!

Thursday 26th

More rain, but good news: Hill says that Mr Bingley and his two sisters are to take up residence at Netherfield tomorrow! I wonder if Charlotte has heard the news.

Friday 27th

For lack of any better occupation, Lydia and Kitty made Mary an apple pie bed yesterday. She was not amused and at breakfast she lectured them upon the sins of idleness and frivolity. Oh la, they have to pass the time somehow.

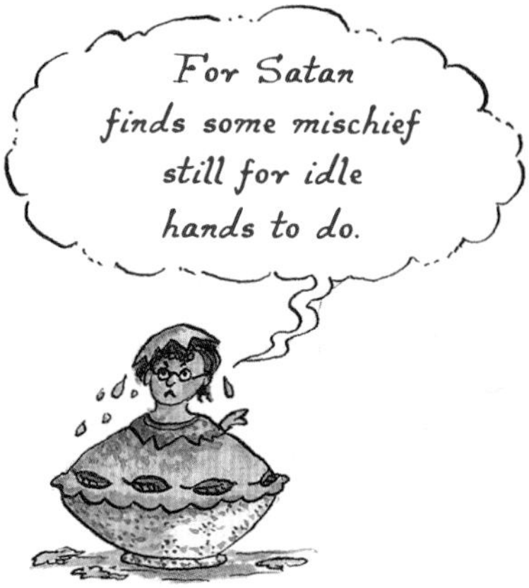

For Satan finds some mischief still for idle hands to do.

Saturday 28th

Mama has already started to nag Papa about calling on Mr Bingley. She is very vexing and Papa just ignores her. Sometimes I fancy that Papa spends too much of his time in books and ignores life altogether.

Life is more ordered in books, Lizzy.

I shall never ignore life.
I plan to fall in
and out of love
at least a dozen times.

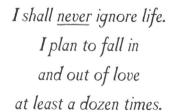

I had hoped this would be my first opportunity to fall in love, for I am already twenty years old and it is time I made a start. Yet if Papa is too stubborn, we may never meet the gentleman. Besides, Jane will capture the first heart to ride this way. Both her countenance and manner are much more pleasing than mine. Well, just a touch more pleasing...

Sunday 29th

I had a good look at myself in the mirror last night, and I fear that even by candlelight Jane is prettier than me. Yet I have fine eyes, a quick wit and am certainly a fairer judge of character than Jane, for she sees nothing but good in everyone. Still, I may have to be content with the second gentleman to ride this way!

This morning Jane and I passed the time painting portraits of each other. I think hers is a fair likeness of me. Although – perhaps my neck is a little longer and my nose a little shorter.

I started cutting out Papa's waistcoat. It is in the finest cream silk and will be lined in blue satin. I am going to cover it in butterflies, flowers and insects!

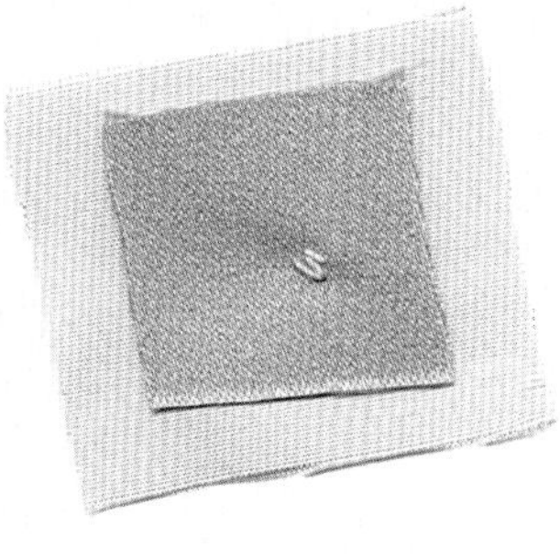

OCTOBER

<u>Tuesday 8th</u>

Dearest Diary,

News at last! We woke to find the rain had vanished, leaving a blue, brisk autumn day with scudding clouds. After breakfast, Jane and I walked across the fields to a hill above Netherfield. We hid amongst the trees as two gentlemen rode by. One looked very merry, the other looked extremely proud and disagreeable. I trust the haughty one is not Mr Bingley for I could never love such a man – and I certainly would not allow Jane to.

I have just painted this picture of Netherfield Park and the unknown gentlemen. I must admit to liking the dog. I could never marry a gentleman who didn't like dogs.

<u>Wednesday 9th</u>

OH, MY PAPA!

Oh Diary,

Our local newspaper.

The Meryton Courier

My Papa is really very teasing! He hid behind his newspaper for the better part of the afternoon. He appeared to ignore Mama as she ranted at him for not calling on Mr Bingley. Then, just as I thought the bonnet I was trimming might fly out of my hands and hit Mama over the head, Papa announced that he had called on Mr Bingley that very morning!

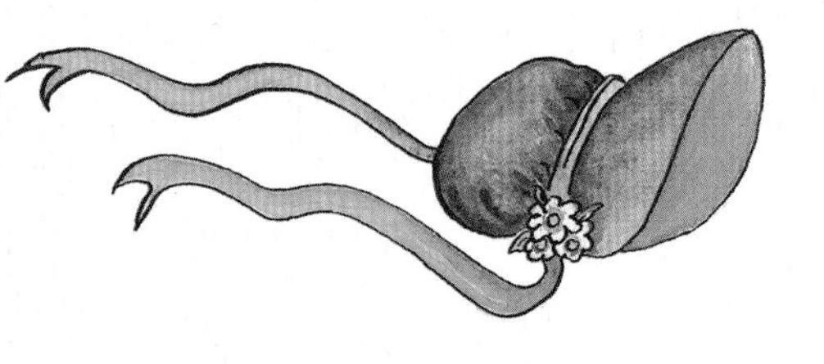

I do hope Mr Bingley returns the call soon. I long to know if he is the merry gentleman or the haughty one. Also, will he come to the ball shortly to be held at the Meryton assembly rooms? And who will he dance with? Lydia is certain it will be her, for although she is the youngest and in my opinion the silliest, she is the tallest. If he has a sharp wit it may be me, but I have little real doubt that it will be Jane.

This is the fur and ribbon I chose for my winter bonnet — is it not delightful? I think that it will set off my eyes to perfection.

When I was younger my favourite poem was about eyes — it is by Robert Herrick and I can still remember it:

UPON HER EYES

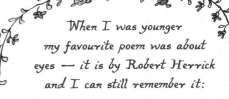

Cleere are her eyes,
Like purest skies,
Discovering from thence
A Babie there
That turns each Sphere,
Like an Intelligence.

Monday 14th

Mr Bingley called on Papa today! Jane and I spied him out of our bedroom window and I am delighted to report that he is the merry one. He wore a blue coat and rode a black horse – so elegant. Imagine if he had seen us hiding behind the curtains! Mama invited him to dinner, but he is returning to London to gather a party for the Meryton ball. I hope there may be more young gentlemen than ladies in his party!

NOVEMBER

Monday 4th

My dear Diary,

I have been neglecting you! Preparations for the Meryton ball have been taking all my time. My own were quickly dispatched, but Lydia and Kitty need much attention.

This is Lydia's dress. Mama has approved it, but I think it is too revealing for she has only just turned fifteen.

NOVEMBER
1811

A WEEK *of* AMUSEMENTS *at the* MERYTON ASSEMBLY ROOMS

Tomorrow is THE day and it is to be hoped that once the ball is over I shall have much news to relate!

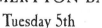

THE MERYTON BALL

Tuesday 5th

Dearest Diary,

It is late, but I cannot sleep without telling you of the great wrong I suffered tonight!

I HAVE HAD A MOST DISAGREEABLE EVENING.

Mr Bingley

Miss Bingley

Mr Bingley, who is all charm, arrived with his two sisters. Caroline Bingley is unmarried and exceedingly haughty. The other, Mrs Hurst, is married to the dull and portly Mr Hurst.

They were accompanied by Mr Bingley's friend, Mr Darcy, the disagreeable gentleman that I saw riding near Netherfield.

Mrs Hurst

Divine.
So fine.
Mine.
No, mine!

Mr Hurst

The other ladies at the ball seemed much taken by Mr Darcy at first, for he has a large estate in Derbyshire and above ten thousand a year. However, they soon came to their senses, for unlike Mr Bingley who was friendly with all, Mr D. was forbidding and proud.

Mr Darcy

Due to the scarcity of gentlemen, I was obliged to sit out for two dances. I was quite happy watching Jane capture Mr Bingley's heart and Kitty and Lydia flirt in every direction. Then I overheard Mr Bingley trying to persuade Mr Darcy to dance with me. Mr Bingley even pointed out how pretty I looked! Well, apparently not pretty enough to tempt Mr Darcy, for he just stuck his nose up in the air and said that he was "in no humour to give consequence to young ladies who are slighted by other men".

Dearest Diary,

Is he not the rudest and most insufferable of men? My defence shall be to laugh at him, but the truth is the bee has stung my pride.

LATER STILL

Our candle is guttering so I must make haste but, as I suspected, Jane is much taken by Mr Bingley and he by her. Well, she has certainly liked many a stupider person. It is just a shame that he doesn't choose his friends more wisely and that his sisters are so proud and conceited.

Jane now pretends to sleep, but I suspect she dreams of dancing with Mr Bingley again! I shall dream of sticking pins into Mr Darcy and bursting his puffed up pride! If he thinks that ten thousand a year and an estate in Derbyshire is an excuse for bad manners, he is much mistaken.

Your slighted friend, Lizzy Bennet.

Wednesday 6th

THE VERY NEXT MORNING

Dear Charlotte and her mother, Mrs Lucas, have just called to talk over the ball. We all agreed that Mr Darcy was exceedingly proud. Mama will not forgive him for refusing to dance with me.

Mary reflected that a person may be proud without being vain. One might wish Mary would keep her reflections to herself.

HERE ENDETH ALL TALK OF THE MERYTON BALL!

Thursday 7th A PAINFUL VISIT

A waistcoat flower

There are times when I wonder how a man as intelligent as my Papa could have married Mama! I suppose she was once quite handsome. She made us call upon the ladies of Netherfield this morning and it was mortifying. Mama was all airs and graces and boasted that our country society was far superior to society in London. She was so pretentious and silly — not that this excuses the Bingley sisters' disdainful treatment of all except Jane. The rest of us seemed to offend their nostrils.

Mr Bingley is altogether different. He is charming to everyone, even Mama. It is clear that he is close to being very much in love with Jane! It is evident to me that his feelings are returned by my sister, but she is all modesty and keeps her feelings hidden.

Even the peacocks of Netherfield took against us!

Friday 8th

Oh fie, Charlotte has just paid me a visit. She thinks I should encourage Jane to let her feelings be better known to Mr Bingley lest he become discouraged. Charlotte believes that Jane must secure Mr Bingley first and then she may fall in love or not as she chooses!

This is the advice of someone who fears she may never marry. Although Charlotte does not like me to mention it, she is already twenty-seven years old — nearly ten years my senior!

Charlotte as a cross old maid with a pack of cross old pugs!

Monday 11th — DINNER WITH THE LUCAS FAMILY

Such very superior dancing...

Sir William Lucas

Today we dined with the Lucases, along with the Bingleys, Mr Darcy and Colonel Forster who commands the local Meryton regiment. The Colonel brought along some of his red-coated officers who quite turned the silly heads of Lydia and Kitty.

The officers of the Shire

Mr Bingley had eyes for none but Jane. Miss Bingley shared her scorn for our country society with Mr Darcy. I ignored them and "kept my breath to cool my porridge" as they say hereabouts. I do believe that they deserve each other, for she is as attached to the use of her arrogant tongue as he is to the view down his aristocratic nose.

I have much affection for porridge but none for aristocratic noses!

Tuesday 12th

I am exceedingly fond of toast.

I smell toast. Yet, in spite of our room being icy without a fire, I hesitate to go down for breakfast. Kitty and Lydia are sure to regale me with details of every redcoat they met last night. Like dear Papa, I have become convinced that they are two of the silliest girls in the Shire.

La, any one of them might turn my head.
I adore the one with blue eyes.
His curls are quite delightful.
They lodge in Meryton.
We must visit Meryton.

Snippets of Kitty and Lydia's mindless midnight chatter as heard through the bedroom wall.

AFTER BREAKFAST

It was hard to know who to sit next to!

It was as I thought, not a word of sense over breakfast. My empty-headed sisters plan to visit Meryton today for the express purpose of happening upon the redcoats. Mama encourages them, which is not to be supported for they are both too young and untamed.

Unlike me, Jane is a fine horsewoman.

Now I am left alone and out of sorts as Jane has gone to spend the day at Netherfield with the Bingley sisters. She had to leave on horseback as Mama forbade Papa to lend her the carriage. Mama hopes for rain, so that Jane will have to stay over and thus have more time to capture Mr Bingley's heart. Shall I be so contriving if I have a daughter?

I wonder the Bingley sisters did not invite me. Not that I would have gone. I suppose I am too countrified for them. I trust they will not find fault with Jane too and come between her and Mr Bingley, for there never was a girl more deserving of good fortune.

The farm cat has had four little kittens. She is most disgruntled!

LATER

Mama got her wish: it has rained all day and Jane has not returned. I must to bed without the cosiness of her company. It has been altogether a most disagreeable day. I even had to unpick a flower on Papa's waistcoat. Oh, I should have written a novel, for I see that life is most disobliging. Just when you think it is going to get better – it gets worse!

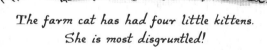

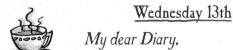

Wednesday 13th

My dear Diary,

I write this from Jane's bedside at Netherfield. Breakfast was scarcely over when this note was delivered.

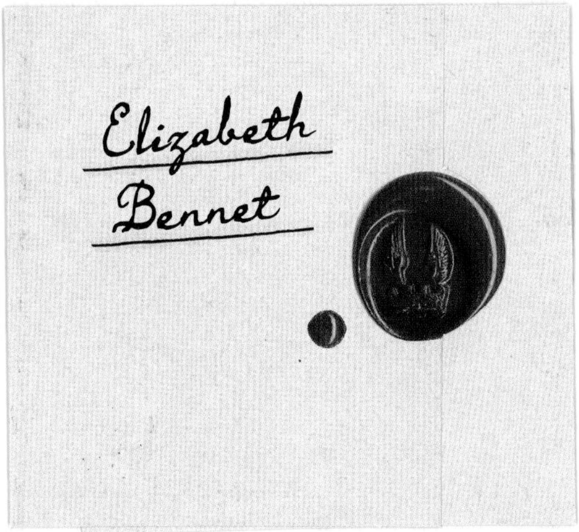
Elizabeth Bennet

My poor Jane. Mama seemed unmoved, even though Jane's illness had been brought on in pursuit of Mr Bingley and under her orders, but I set out for Netherfield at once. I had to walk three miles across boggy fields and I arrived with mud up to my knees!

The family and Mr Darcy were still at breakfast. They all greeted me with contempt, except Mr Bingley, who was charm itself, and Mr Hurst who just kept eating! It is obviously not done in polite circles to walk in the mud and on one's own. Well, I don't give an aristocratic jot for their sensibilities – the fact is that Jane is not at all well.

The coddler and egg cups were silver.

She has been very restless all morning, but is now asleep. I hate to leave her, but I must set off for home before it gets dark.

LATER

When Jane became agitated at parting with me, Miss Bingley grudgingly invited me to remain at Netherfield. I accepted!

A servant is even now dispatched to collect a supply of clothes. Lord, how plain I shall look at dinner amidst all the grandeur.

Your rags, Miss Elizabeth.

AFTER DINNER

Soup

Jelly

If it were not for Jane I would leave this instant! Dinner was a most uncomfortable affair. Mr Darcy spoke only to challenge my wit, which I might say is a sure match for his!

Game pie

Custards

Miss Bingley seemed to find any attention paid to me by Mr Darcy most painful. She makes every effort to gain it and I make none!

Nuts

Ices

I escaped back to Jane as soon as dinner was finished. She seems worse rather than better. I think I shall stay by her tonight.

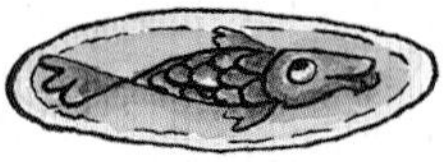

Trout

Mr Bingley is truly concerned. His sisters are solacing their concern by playing duets – badly!

Thursday 14th

Dearest Diary,

I feel very alone. Jane is no better and the Bingley sisters are most unpleasant company. They scorn all but Jane.

Dear Mr Bingley has just sent the housemaid with a jug of winter berries to cheer Jane. I have put them by her bed and I will pass the afternoon painting them.

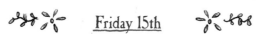

Friday 15th

If it were not for the company, I could get used to the luxury of Netherfield. The rooms are always warm and servants always at hand. From our bedroom window we can see far across the estate. It looks so beautiful under its blanket of hoar frost.

Jane is now out of bed and sitting by the fire. Mr Bingley has sent a note expressing his delight.

I hope she may come downstairs soon, as meals are torture. Mr Darcy has abandoned the view down his nose and taken to staring at me. It is most discomposing and I can only suppose that I have committed some reprehensible wrong.

Today I added this Netherfield thistle to Papa's waistcoat. Mr Bingley is the flower and his family and friends the thorns. The largest thorn is Mr Darcy!

ANOTHER EVENING OF TORTURE!

After dinner, Jane came down to the drawing room, which should have made the evening more bearable, but Mr Bingley took all her attention. Mr Darcy and I conversed on character defects. I declared his to be a propensity to hate everybody. He declared mine to be a willful misunderstanding of everyone. What say you to that, dear Diary?

This is Bingo. He belongs to Mr Bingley and is my good friend.

BLESSED SATURDAY!

Dearest Diary,

Lord, how happy I am! Jane is much better and we are to return home. I have sent word to Mama to send the carriage. We are both wrapped and ready to go.

BAD NEWS

Mama has just sent this note refusing us the carriage. Now we are trapped here until tomorrow. Only for Jane's sake will I suffer it.

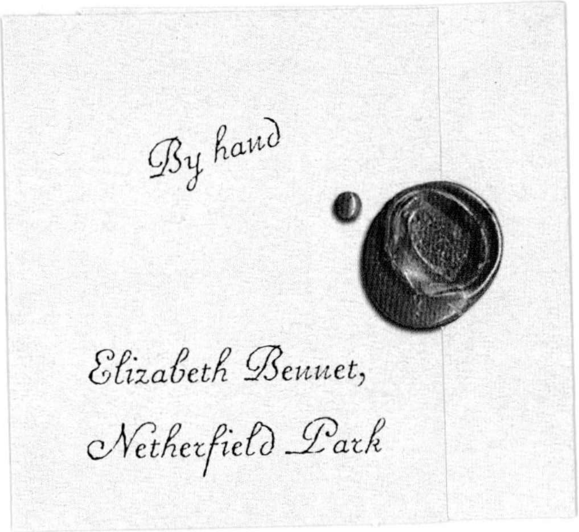
By hand

Elizabeth Bennet,
Netherfield Park

MOST BLESSED SUNDAY

May the bells ring out!

My dear Diary,

Home at last! The Netherfield company were most cordial on our departure. Their delight at our leaving must have caused a sudden rush of civility. Mama greeted us with less civility. She is rarely pleased to see me and would have Jane return only when engaged to Mr Bingley. I believe Papa is glad I am home as his nose appeared out of his book for quite two minutes! Our sisters are indifferent – Mary is busy studying the piano and human nature, and as for Kitty and Lydia – their minds are still empty of all but redcoats!

Redcoats in varying sizes!

Monday 18th

At breakfast, Papa gave me this letter to read out. It is from Mr Collins, the unloved cousin who will inherit Papa's estate!

Hunsford,
near Westerham,
Kent
15 October

Mr Bennet,
Longbourn,
near Meryton

How like Papa to let us have the news at the very last instant. Mama's nerves are not improved by the imminent arrival of the gentleman who may one day throw us from our home. As to making amends, there is nothing he can do that will satisfy Mama.

Could Mr Collins be the second gentleman to ride this way? I doubt it, for he sounds a real oddity. I suspect Papa thinks some amusement may be had at his expense.

I gave half my toast to a robin this morning.

LATE EVENING

I never was so glad to escape to my bedroom. Mr Collins arrived on the dot of four o'clock and is exceedingly ... well, exceedingly everything! He is twenty-five years old, tall, heavy-featured and nearly as stout as I had imagined.

A quick sketch of Mr C.

He converses with an air of great solemnity especially when talking of his benefactor Lady Catherine de Bourgh, her daughter, or their Rosings Park estate. He calls us his "fair cousins" and tries to flatter us, but he upset Mama greatly by regarding the house as though it were already his. He also asked her which of his "fair cousins" had cooked supper. Mama left him in little doubt that we were well able to employ a cook!

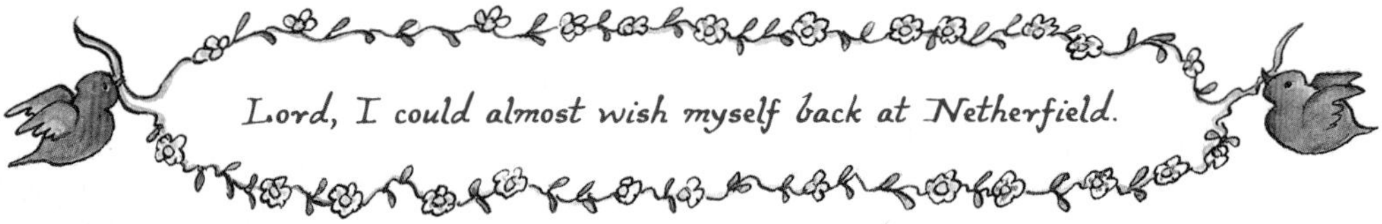

Lord, I could almost wish myself back at Netherfield.

Tuesday 19th

Flowers are a blessing!

My dear Diary,

I am already marking the days until Mr C. leaves us! Papa is taking pleasure in making him appear absurd. Mr C. gave us each a gift of a prayer card. I wonder at mine, for some days my blessings seem few.

Give us a thankful sense of the Blessings in which we live, Almighty Father.

Jane Austen

Oh la, another ink splash!

LATER IN BED

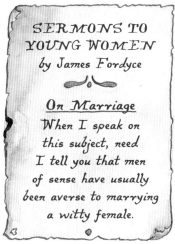

SERMONS TO YOUNG WOMEN
by James Fordyce

On Marriage
When I speak on this subject, need I tell you that men of sense have usually been averse to marrying a witty female.

Lord, what chance has Lizzy Bennet of being wed?!

Jane chides me for being too hard on Mr Collins (and for getting ink on the sheets), but I will never have her ability to find good in everyone. After dinner Mr Collins sought to entertain us by reading "Fordyce's Sermons". Well, for once I blessed Lydia's frivolous mind. After three agonizing pages of Fordyce, she interrupted his flow with more news of the redcoats. Most especially of Mr Denny, her current favourite! Mr C. was amazed for he knows little of young ladies such as our Lydia.

As I write this Jane is brushing her hair. Her eyes tell me that she dreams of Mr Bingley. I wonder that he has not yet come to enquire about her.

And so to sleep.

Wednesday 20th

Dearest Diary,

I write in haste for we are off to Meryton, yet I must tell you what I just overheard.

Make haste, turn the page!

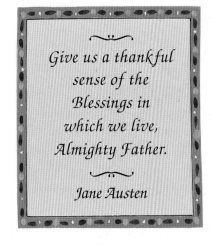

My parsonage house stands in need of a mistress!

That looks a likely goose!

Mr Collins made it known to Mama that he wishes to make amends for inheriting Longbourn by marrying one of her daughters! Lord, he talked as if he were choosing a goose to keep his lawn trim, for he expressed no preference as to which daughter.

Mama, of course, was delighted. She said she felt bound to mention that her eldest was likely to be engaged soon, but her younger daughters had no attachments. All this ***BEFORE*** *breakfast!*

I could not eat a crumb of toast. I fear that as I am next in age to Jane, our cousin might pick me. He is not a sensible man! He is by turns proud, obsequious, self-important and humble. I could never love such a man. Besides, Kent is too great a distance from Longbourn. Oh! I will not give him the slightest reason to be encouraged.

LATER

Papa has already bored of Mr Collins. He persuaded him to accompany "his fair cousins" into Meryton. I tried to be politely distant as he expounded on the wonders of Rosings Park. Luckily, when we reached Meryton, Lydia caught sight of Mr Denny and his new friend, Mr George Wickham.

What a charming pink nose, Miss Elizabeth.
It was icy cold and I knew my nose must be red.

Mr Wickham was a delightful surprise.
Oh yes, indeed he was.

He is about to join the regiment and, I have to say, regimentals will do nothing if not improve his charm, for he is very handsome. He is taller than Mr Denny and his countenance and manner are greatly in his favour!

I was quite put out when we were interrupted by the arrival of Mr Bingley and Mr Darcy. They had been on their way to Longbourn to enquire after Jane, which made her blush most fetchingly.

These are to go on Papa's waistcoat. They are Adonis Blue, his favourite butterflies.

The progression of Jane's blush!

I was astonished by the strangeness of the meeting between Mr Darcy and Mr Wickham. Both appeared most agitated. One turned white and the other red and neither deigned a salutation. It is impossible to imagine the meaning of this, but I long to know and WILL find out!

We went on to our aunt, Mrs Philips. She is to invite the officers to dine with us tomorrow! I am all eagerness to see Mr Wickham again and also to discover more of the awkwardness between him and Mr Darcy.

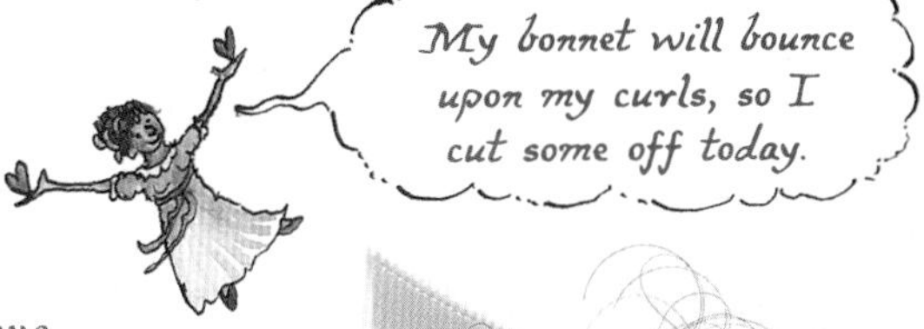

My bonnet will bounce upon my curls, so I cut some off today.

Thursday 21st

My dearest Diary,

I hope that you will forgive me: I believe that I have momentarily become as empty-headed and self-concerned as Lydia. I have spent much if not all the day thinking of Mr Wickham!

The small remainder of the day was spent avoiding Mr Collins and attending to my hair and clothes for tonight. Really, Lizzy, this will not do. La, I have another whole hour to wait before the carriage takes us to Meryton and Mr Wickham.

♥ LATE EVENING

Oh and oh again, Jane has fallen asleep and I have an urgent desire to talk over the evening. My early admiration for Mr Wickham was not in the smallest degree unreasonable. All the ladies' eyes were upon him, but he sat by ME! I vow that he grew handsomer as every second passed. He also revealed more than I could have hoped of the reason for the strange greeting between him and Mr Darcy.

The Tale of Mr Darcy's Black-Hearted Deed!

Related by George Wickham (The injured party)

Is it not shocking? I knew I was right not to like Mr Darcy. Mr Wickham says that Mr Darcy has a sister, Georgiana, who is just fifteen years old but already as proud and prejudiced as her brother.

I was all astonishment that Mr Bingley could have such a friend. My astonishment grew still greater when, thanks to Mr Collins' constant references to Lady Catherine de Bourgh, I discovered that Mr Darcy is that lady's nephew!

Lady C. this...
Lady C. that...
Lady C. this...
Lady C. that...
Lady C, Lady C!

Mr Wickham says that Mr Darcy is expected to marry his cousin, Miss de Bourgh. Ha, vain indeed are all Miss Bingley's attentions to him. No, I smile not – or only a little!

Think not, dear Diary, that my heart is bent
in George Wickham's favour,
for it is certain!
Tonight Jane will not be the only one dreaming dreams!

Avoided Mr C. all evening!

Pussy Mama ran by us with a mouse!

Friday 22nd

After breakfast I walked with Jane in the shrubbery to discuss last night's revelations. Jane would not believe that Mr Darcy could be so unworthy of Mr Bingley's regard. She did not see the truth in Mr Wickham's looks as I did. Oh, will my dear sister never think ill of anybody?!

We were interrupted by the arrival of Mr Bingley and his sisters. They brought an invitation to a ball at Netherfield. A most pleasing prospect as I shall be able to dance with Mr Wickham!

I believe that Mr Bingley would have lingered at Jane's side all day, for he could scarcely take his eyes from her, but his sisters could not wait to leave us!

Mr Charles Bingley
requests the pleasure of
THE BENNET FAMILY at a BALL
to be held at
NETHERFIELD PARK
on 26 November 1811 at 6 p.m.
Carriages at 11 p.m.
RSVP

My favourite dance is the gavotte.

LATE AFTERNOON

Oh, I wish to scream! Mr Collins, who unfortunately has no religious objection to dancing, has solicited the first two dances from me. The very two I had hoped to share with Mr Wickham!

It would have been uncivil to refuse, but I hope it does not give him reason to suppose that I could ever contemplate being mistress of his parsonage.

Kitty and Lydia are thoroughly overexcited at the prospect of a ball.

LATE EVENING

Jane is already abed. She has developed a sweet love-smile. I have developed a hunted look, for I am now certain that I am the prey of Mr Collins. He hovers in every doorway with a "delicate little compliment" for me. Mama hinted that my engagement to HIM would be exceedingly agreeable to her. Not to me, Mama, I can assure you. Let one of my other sisters save Longbourn for you, for I never shall.

Jane and I share our bed with the cats.

Sunday 24th

It has started to snow. I trust this will not mean the ball will be cancelled. Mr C. is like a vexing puppy, always underfoot and squirming. I am trying to concentrate on creating a bandeau for my hair. It matches my gown and will sparkle as I dance with a certain young officer, while tossing scornful glances at the owner of an aristocratic nose. Oh, happy dream!

Monday 25th

The snow has settled. Even Kitty and Lydia abandoned their visit to Meryton.

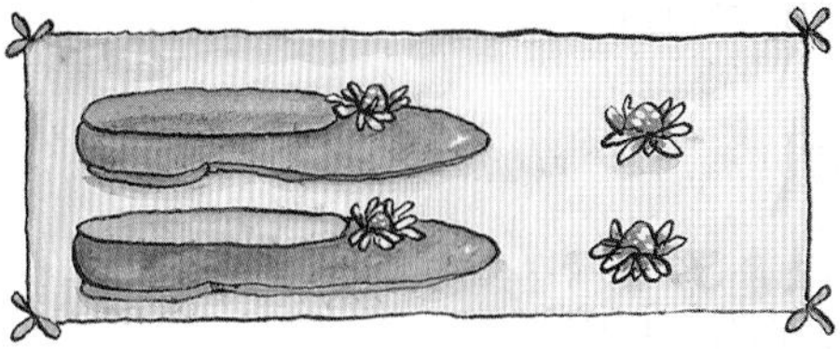

Hill kindly collected our shoe roses from the haberdasher's. She returned with a pink nose and frozen toes! My roses are blue and white satin and I think they look perfect. I plan to be irresistible!

THE DAY OF THE NETHERFIELD BALL!

Tuesday 26th

TEA TIME

Papa has at last declared that it is safe to travel by carriage! Kitty, Lydia and Mama have been in a fever of anxiety all day – which is not to say that I haven't been secretly concerned!

Mary has given me a pounding headache by practising the piano without stopping. She hopes she may be asked to play tonight – I trust not.

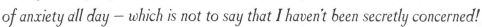

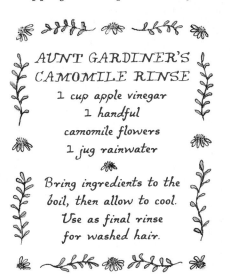

AUNT GARDINER'S CAMOMILE RINSE

1 cup apple vinegar
1 handful camomile flowers
1 jug rainwater

Bring ingredients to the boil, then allow to cool. Use as final rinse for washed hair.

Jane and I have washed each other's hair in camomile, which makes it shine wondrously.

Neither of us has eaten a morsel for excitement. It is now time to get dressed. Oh, I do hope, dear Diary, that I shall have much George Wickham news to relate to you in a few hours time!

PS – Jane has just said that I look exceedingly pretty. I am not vain, but I do believe she may be right. Oh, it is time to leave!

MISERY AT NETHERFIELD

New resolution: refuse all invitations to balls!

At least the food was agreeable.

My dear Diary,

I left you in the highest of spirits and return in the lowest. This is why:

1. Mr Wickham was not at the ball. I suspect he was avoiding Mr Darcy. I was mortified. My new shoe roses and bandeau were utterly wasted!

2. I had to dance with Mr Collins. This did nothing to revive my spirits. He kept moving the wrong way and then apologizing instead of attending to the next step. He is embarrassing and ridiculous.

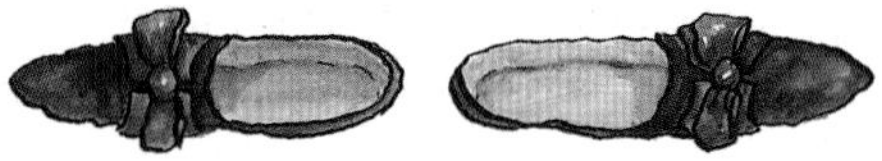

3. Mr Darcy asked me to dance! He approached me without warning and I was so overcome by surprise that I forgot my resolution and agreed. I felt most disloyal to Mr Wickham, yet much amazed that Mr Darcy had paid me the compliment after his behaviour at the Meryton ball! However, half an hour of dancing with Mr Darcy is a challenge I do not wish to repeat. He has no grace and made no effort at conversation. I tried to tease him into talking, but he was not to be drawn. I was never more relieved than when the music finished.

ORDER OF DANCES	ORDER OF DANCES
1. Chassé Mr Collins	5. Le Boulanger Colonel Forster
2. Fleuret Mr Collins	6. Minuet Mr Miles
3. Gavotte Mr Darcy	7. Country dance Mr Charles
4. Cotillion Mr Darcy	8. La Belle Assemblée Mr Denny

My dance card — witness to every ballroom trial.

4. Miss Bingley was her usual vain, disagreeable self. She made a point of telling me that Mr Darcy had been remarkably kind to George Wickham, in spite of that gentleman's infamous behaviour. She couldn't say what infamous behaviour, so I saw her off with an icy retort.

5. Mama boasted to the whole ballroom that Jane and Mr Bingley would soon be married. I saw Mr Darcy flinch at the thought.

6. Mary played the piano badly and for too long.

I will not even mention Mr C.'s attentions or the fact that Mama ordered the carriage quite some quarter of an hour after everyone else left. Such was the Bingley sisters' desire to be rid of us, they nearly threw us out in the snow!

"We do so hope that you do not freeze to death."

HERE ENDETH MY TALE OF WOE!
MAY TOMORROW BRING SOME SUNSHINE.

Wednesday 27th

OH!

No sunshine – more like thunder and lightning! I have received a proposal of marriage and I'm sure you can guess from whom! Well, I shall tell you.

IT HAPPENED LIKE THIS

Scarcely had we finished breakfast than Mr Collins contrived to be alone with me. I tried to make my escape, but he and Mama trapped me. He then started on such a discourse that I could hardly refrain from laughing. Yet it was no laughing matter for it was evident he was making a serious proposal of marriage. Yes, it is true!

MR COLLINS PROPOSED MARRIAGE TO ME!
Me, of all people, has the man no sense?!

It seems he only wants to marry because he was advised to do so by the "very noble Lady Catherine". He most ungallantly noted my lack of a fortune, yet promised never to let an ungenerous reproach pass his lips. Oh, those lips, imagine them touching my own – the very thought is insupportable!

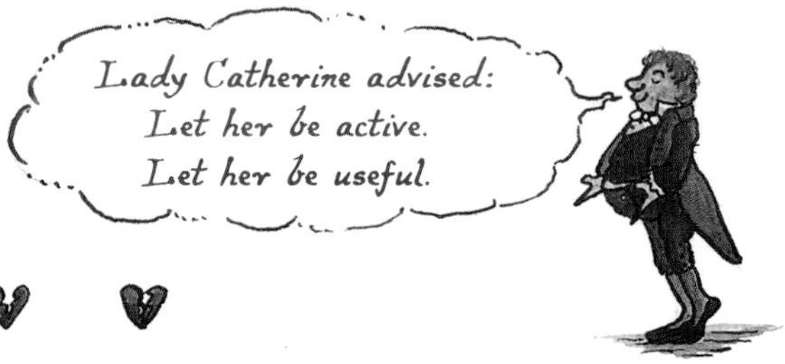

Lady Catherine advised:
Let her be active.
Let her be useful.

Of course, I refused. I called upon Mama to support me, but she declared she will never see me again if I do not marry Mr Collins. Now dear Papa has declared he will never see me again if I DO!

I have retired to my room. I am so utterly discomposed. I will never marry that ridiculous man. Just because I lack a fortune must I also lack love within my marriage?

Oh, now Charlotte has arrived – I had better go and greet her. She will surely understand the horror of my situation!

MY FIRST and most
UNWELCOME PROPOSAL –
Hopefully not my last!
Life is not as I would have it!

A LITTLE LATER

We are all sitting in the parlour and I am still feeling very agitated. Mr Collins does not appear to be suffering from a broken heart. Indeed, the only heart suffering seems to be Mama's. Such an undutiful daughter is not good for her nerves.

Charlotte is being a dear and cheering Mr Collins with her chatter. I had better take up my sewing and sit beside them, lest they ask me what I am writing. Just think, I might have had to exchange embroidering Papa's waistcoat for stitching a hassock!

Thursday 28th

A true gentleman would have returned home after being refused in marriage, but not Mr Collins. He remains to fan Mama's peevishness towards her wayward daughter.

Fiddlesticks, I will not be put out by Mr Collins! The snow has thawed and we are off to Meryton, where I hope to meet with someone much more to my liking. Lydia's idea, not mine, although I fancy I may have buttered it onto her toast at breakfast!

We saw two hares today. They looked thin and cold.

EVENING TROUBLING NEWS

Jane has received a letter from Caroline Bingley. She is very shocked and so am I for the news is bad indeed. The whole party has left Netherfield for London. Miss Bingley makes it clear that she intends to trap her brother in London for the winter. I believe that she sees he is in love with Jane, but intends him to marry Mr Darcy's sister, Georgiana. She probably imagines that this will help her own cause with Mr Darcy. We are not grand or rich enough for them.

Fie upon them!

Jane cannot believe her friend is capable of such deception. Her desire to find good in everyone blinds her to the truth. I wish she would trust in my ability to judge character and in Mr Charles Bingley's true regard for her.

We have not shared this news with Mama lest her nerves completely overcome us. She is planning a dinner for Mr Bingley's return. I have faith that he will be there and that he will then declare his love for Jane.

Mr Wickham left his calling card for Papa. It is in the utmost good taste.

It seems selfish to mention this after poor Jane's news, but we did see Mr Wickham in Meryton today. He was most attentive! He confided that he had not attended the ball for fear of a scene with Mr Darcy. He is so forbearing.

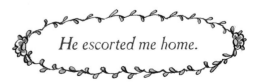

He escorted me home.

Friday 29th AN UNREMARKABLE DAY

Charlotte came over and helped us with Mr Collins. Still no word from Mr Bingley. Jane has sent a reply to Miss Bingley's letter. She did not show it to me, but I feel sure it was more charming than that lady deserves. Even by candlelight I see that Jane's dreams are not as happy as they once were.

Saturday 30th

Praise be, Mr Collins leaves at dawn tomorrow and we have already said our farewells! He vanished all day today, which we felt a great bonus for his company has been trying us all. Neither he nor his esteemed benefactor, Lady Catherine de Bourgh, will be missed one jot!

I hope tomorrow will bring news of both Mr Bingley and Mr W.!

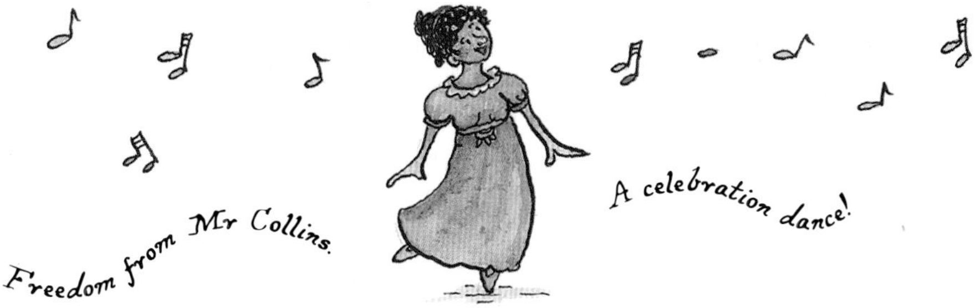

Good night, dear Diary, and good night Mr W. – wherever you are.

This is the border for Papa's waistcoat.

Sunday 1st DECEMBER

Dearest Diary,

If I were writing a novel you would accuse me of straying into the realms of fantasy. You will just not believe this:

CHARLOTTE IS ENGAGED TO MR COLLINS!

Marriage is the only proper provision for a woman of small fortune.

Yesterday, when we were thankful that he was not with us, he was at the Lucases' proposing to Charlotte! She wished to tell me herself, so prevailed upon him not to announce the news before he left.

I had to make a strong effort to wish her happiness, as it will be quite impossible with such a man. I hardly know how she could accept someone who makes two offers of marriage within three days. She says that although Mr Collins' society is irksome, at least she will not die an old maid or be a burden to her family.

I feel sad, for I shall never feel able to be close with Charlotte again. It is intolerable to have a friend who has sacrificed every better feeling for worldly advantage. I trust Mr Wickham will not judge me by my friend the parson's wife!

Mama is outraged and was very rude to Sir William Lucas, as Charlotte will one day be mistress of Longbourn. Lady Lucas is very smug. Mama blames me and scolds me at every opportunity. Papa is delighted as it proves to him that Sir William's daughter is more foolish than his own!

As foolish as my wife, more foolish than my daughter.

Tuesday 3rd

I put out an apple for the birds. They're happy!

I am still unaccountably put out by Charlotte's engagement.

Mama has taken to drawing Mr Bingley's absence to Jane's attention at hourly intervals. Her hopes of seeing at least one daughter married are fading fast. For myself, I still don't doubt Mr Bingley's affection for Jane, but I fear his heartless sisters may have persuaded him to look elsewhere for marriage. Jane appears serene, but I believe she suffers terribly. I would not be able to hide my feelings half so well if Mr Wickham retired to London without a word.

I don't blame YOU Jane — you would have caught Bingley if you could — but LIZZY!

Sunday 8th

My dear Diary,

I have been in bed for the last few days with a troublesome cold. Hill has been most attentive with her suffocating inhalations! This has made it difficult to write, for dear Hill does not appreciate my propensity for getting ink on the sheets!

Now, just as I am recovering, Mr C. is returning to plan his wedding. Mama is exceedingly put out and wonders why he does not stay with the Lucases. For once, Mama and I are in agreement!

It is fortuitous that his lovemaking will require his presence at Lucas Lodge for the greater part of each day – Longbourn is cheerless enough. Jane is quietly miserable and Mama refuses to address me. The silence is only broken by Kitty and Lydia who prattle on without any feeling for others.

Monday 16th

Mr Collins arrived with his usual punctiliousness. Let us hope he leaves in the same manner. I could perhaps forge a letter from his esteemed patroness, recalling him urgently to Rosings!

Oh la, a letter from Lady Catherine.
Oh, my gracious patroness requires my presence! I must fly, I must fly!

Wednesday 18th JANE IS CAST INTO DESPAIR

A BLACK, BLACK DAY.

Jane has received a letter from Caroline Bingley. All hope of Mr Bingley's return is over. Entirely over. Miss Bingley makes it clear that they are settled in London for the winter. She also boasts of her brother's closeness to Miss Darcy.

I am certain that it is Miss Bingley and Mr Darcy who lead Mr Bingley to sacrifice his and Jane's happiness. I can hardly think of them without contempt! They care nothing for love – just money and family connections.

It will surely be a cold, white Christmas!

My poor, dear, sweet Jane. She is one of the few people I truly love, for the more I see of the world, the more dissatisfied I am with it!

Papa makes a joke of the affair and says that now Jane has been jilted it must be my turn. He fancies Mr Wickham would make a fine job of it. Oh my Papa! The truth of it is he just can't face Jane's unhappiness.

He does vex me so.

Saturday 21st

I trust they do not wed in Meryton Church.

Mr Collins has taken his leave. I am not sorry. His marriage plans continue apace and I find the whole idea unaccountable! Mr Collins is a conceited, pompous, narrow-minded man and Charlotte cannot be thinking straight.

Goodbye Mr C. Please do not hurry your return!

Thank every little berry on the mistletoe: my favourite aunt will arrive for Christmas any day now. Surely <u>then</u> I will recover my sense of humour.

Monday 23rd

My dear Diary,

Be of good cheer, my humour has returned! Mama's brother, Mr Gardiner, has arrived bringing with him my lovely aunt and little cousins. Mama will now have someone else to complain to and our little cousins will make it a merry Christmas.

I look forward to introducing my aunt to Mr Wickham for she is sure to be charmed by him.

The Gardiner family

I feel light-hearted once more!

Tuesday 24th

My dear Diary,

It is as I thought – Mrs Gardiner understands everything. She has already prevailed upon Jane to return to London with them after Christmas. We hope that Mr Bingley will hear she is in town and call upon her. At the very least it will give Jane a break from Mama.

Mrs Gardiner is the dearest of aunts. She brought us all the most delightful Christmas presents. I received an array of gorgeous coloured silks for Papa's waistcoat, and she also gave us each a dress length. She tells us that our short-sleeved gowns are sadly out of fashion.

I fancy this
blue will look perfect
with lace trim ...
and long sleeves!

How handsome
Papa will look
in his waistcoat.

Was there ever such a generous reviver of spirits?

Monday 30th

Dearest Diary,

Christmas has flown by in a flurry of social engagements. We have dined and danced, danced and dined! Mr Wickham has been present on each occasion and I sense that he prefers me to every other young lady in Meryton. I continue to find him utterly captivating.

My aunt used to live near Pemberley and knew Mr Darcy's father, so she had much in common with Mr Wickham. She did warn me against getting too fond of him as he lacks an income, but love takes no account of such details. I promised only that I would not insist Mama include him in every invitation. I think I can rely on Lydia to do that! Besides, I am in no hurry to tie myself to one gentleman – there is much to be gained by enjoying one's independence.

Sadly, my aunt has returned to London today, taking Jane with her. My only comfort is that I may soon hear that Jane has been reunited with Mr Bingley. I shall watch for the post daily.

Mr Collins and Charlotte are to be married on Thursday 9 January. I had hoped the ceremony would be in Kent, but it is to be at Meryton Church. Mr Collins is even now arriving at Lucas Lodge to prepare for the event. Mama, who has been in good spirits during my aunt and uncle's visit, has had a return of her nerves.

HERE ENDETH 1811

PRIVATE

The New Year Wishes of Elizabeth Bennet

JANUARY

Wednesday 8th

Charlotte paid us a farewell visit. Mama was so ill-natured that I made an effort to be friendlier than I felt. Charlotte made me promise to visit her in Kent this March, but I take no pleasure in the thought. Although the comfort of intimacy is over between us, I shall miss her company, for there is little enough hereabouts.

Thursday 9th

Such a very superior wedding!

THE WEDDING DAY OF CHARLOTTE AND MR COLLINS

What can I say? Charlotte is now Mrs Collins and everything went as expected. The bride wore a white gown adorned with bows and the groom hardly uttered a word without referring to his most illustrious patron, Lady Catherine de Bourgh. She did not do him the honour of attending, which was one blessing! It snowed.

Friday 10th

My dear Diary,

Lord, what a strange mood I am in. My best friend married to a gentleman who knows as little about love as a herring and my dearest sister gone away to nurse a broken heart. I shall have to cheer myself up by persuading Mama to invite a certain gentleman to dinner. La, life may not be completely over...

Dear Mr Wickham, Please make all haste to
Longbourn before our Lizzy expires of boredom.
Yours, Mrs Bennet.

Monday 13th

Truly, thirteen is an unlucky number. I have received a letter from Jane, which convinces me that Caroline Bingley is determined not to let her brother know that Jane is in London. When she called on Miss Bingley and Mrs Hurst they were most unfriendly, and made a point of telling her that Mr Bingley was always with Mr Darcy and his sister, Georgiana. My heart aches for my lovely sister.

My heart will ache even more if I don't see Mr W. soon.

Tuesday 14th

My dear Diary,

I am most concerned by Lydia's behaviour. She is spending too much time flirting with the young officers and encouraging Kitty to do likewise. I wonder Papa does not warn her that her conduct is unbecoming to a young lady of her age, or indeed any age.

"La, Kitty, which officer shall we declare the most handsome?"

Jane is ever in my thoughts. Her unhappiness and the cruelty of the Bingley sisters even mars my enjoyment of Mr Wickham's company. Not that I have seen much of him recently. Between you and me, dearest Diary, there are rumours that he has turned his attention elsewhere, but I am quite persuaded of his loyalty to me! Just imagine, though: if I had married Mr Collins I would not even have the luxury of speculating about such matters.

My new gown

I shall wear my new long-sleeved dress and a feather in my hair when next I see him – that will surely stop his gaze wandering!

This is the border for the back of Papa's waistcoat. The last winter berries that I painted were picked for my dear Jane by Mr Bingley. How long ago that seems!

FEBRUARY

Saturday 1st

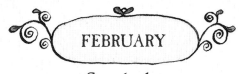

My dearest Diary,

Almost a month has elapsed since I wrote last. During that time my expectations and my pride have taken a knock. The rumours were all true and Mr Wickham has cast me aside for another. Her name is Miss King, a quite unremarkable person by all accounts. However, she recently inherited a fortune, and if anyone is in need of a fortune, it is Mr Wickham.

In truth, I have found it impossible to write about this until now. At first I was very shocked, but I am slowly starting to feel free of hurt. After the terrible disappointments Mr Wickham has suffered at the hands of Mr Darcy, I find his pursuit of financial security hurtful but understandable.

Naturally, Mama takes Mr Wickham's new interest as a personal slight. Her nerves and her dislike of me seem to be boundless. I do miss Jane, for Papa is certainly not interested in discussing affairs of the heart. I also miss weaving my nightly dreams of Mr W. but I am determined to remain optimistic. I do believe that another young gentleman will one day come riding my way!

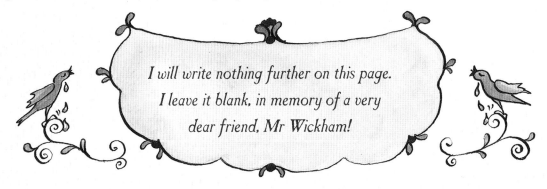

I will write nothing further on this page.
I leave it blank, in memory of a very
dear friend, Mr Wickham!

PS – I must remember to tell my aunt that not even long-sleeved gowns always have the desired result!

Tuesday 4th

My dear Diary,

I have received the most distressing letter from Jane. She has not seen Mr Bingley and Caroline Bingley has only just returned her call, briefly and without warmth.

I read bits of Jane's letter to Papa. He believes Jane is too good for the Bingley family!

My only comfort is that Jane at last knows Charlotte Bingley's true nature. As for Mr Bingley, I can no longer hold him in high regard. If Mr Wickham's account of Miss Darcy is correct, I trust she will make him as unhappy as he has made my good sister. I am rapidly going off all men. I find my heart is still bruised, although I maintain a cheerful countenance!

Saturday 15th

Dear Diary,

I have not been paying you the attention you deserve. I fear that life at Longbourn is again disturbed only by domestic inconveniences and Mama's nerves! I even begin to look forward to my visit to Charlotte, especially as it now includes a night with Jane on the way. I shall be sorry to leave Papa, but that is all.

I think that I will walk into Meryton next week to take my farewell of Mr Wickham. I just need to be certain that he is still bent on seeking a fortune instead of love!

A fox got into the hen house this morning. It ate all the egg layers. How did it know?!

Papa's geese love this weather.

Sunday 1st

Dear Diary,

The weather has been so cold, dirty and disagreeable that I have hardly left the house. We managed to go to church today, so I think tomorrow I will finally venture into Meryton.

Monday 2nd

Kitty and Lydia accompanied me into Meryton. We were practically blown there by a March wind! We met Mr Wickham and some of the other officers and passed a pleasant hour with them at my Aunt Philips' house.

Mr Wickham walked us home and we parted on good terms. It seems he is still bent on pursuing Miss King, but I will always think of him as amiable and have no regrets. Lydia seems a little less eager to forgive him for chasing ten thousand a year instead of a Bennet sister!

I said farewell to Papa this evening, for we are to leave for London early tomorrow. I will miss him and I think that he will miss me. He even promised to write to me! I shall take his waistcoat and try to finish it before my return.

My bonnet blew away! Kitty and Lydia thought it most amusing. Mr Wickham caught it for me.

LONDON

My little cousins!

My aunt's house in Gracechurch Street.

Tuesday 3rd

Yes, I am in London!

Sir William and Maria, Charlotte's father and sister, collected me at dawn. Sir William was knighted by the King while mayor of Meryton – he is very self-important! Luckily the rattle of the carriage drowned most of his grandiose prattle.

We arrived in London around noon and received such a welcome from Jane, my little cousins and Mr and Mrs Gardiner. What a joy to be with them and to see that Jane has not become ill with sorrow – although my aunt says that she has periods of great dejection.

I told Jane about Wickham transferring his affections to Miss King. She does not really understand his behaviour as I do. Nor does my aunt, who wonders he showed Miss King no attention until she inherited some money.

Wednesday 4th

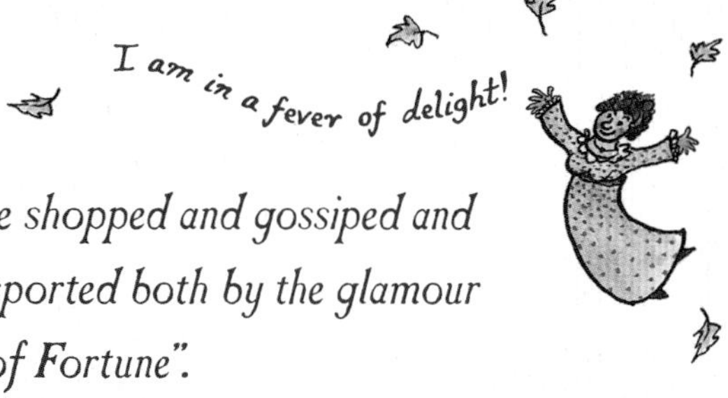

Dearest Diary,

We have had such a day! This morning we shopped and gossiped and this evening we went to the theatre. I was transported both by the glamour of the audience and by the play, "The Wheel of Fortune".

I love London. It has healed my heart and I find my enthusiasm for life has quite returned. I also have a wonderful treat to look forward to: in the summer I am to travel to the Lake District with my aunt and uncle! Oh la, what are men compared to lakes and mountains?

I can write no more now, for these are my last minutes with Jane – tomorrow we travel on to Hunsford. Tonight I have someone to warm my cold toes against and whisper my secrets to! I hope I will leave my sister a little happier, even if she is unable to put all thoughts of Mr Bingley behind her!

A FEW MEMORIES OF LONDON

A map of the district around Gracechurch Street.

Harding Howell and Co. at Pall Mall. My aunt's favourite shop!

I bought the buttons for Papa's waistcoat. They had such a selection! I bought this spare one as a memento.

My dear aunt is so kind and generous. She treated Jane and me to a new pair of evening gloves and a bonnet each!

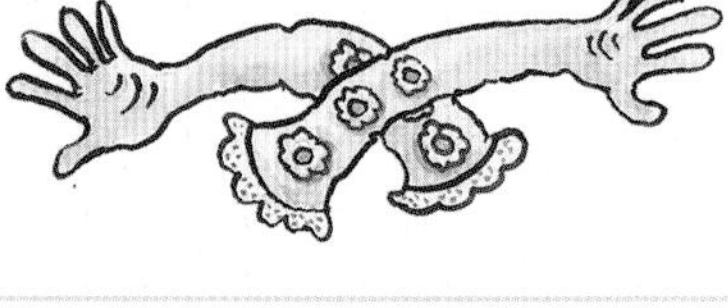

A receipt for some shoe roses I bought for Kitty, Lydia and Mary.

HALL AND ALAN

Date: 4 March 1812

Received of: Miss Elizabeth Bennet

The sum of: four shillings for six shoe roses.

Fie, how dull Kent will seem after London!

I am still in a fever of delight.

My aunt has as many dogs as she has children.

THEATRE ROYAL COVENT GARDEN

This present WEDNESDAY, 4 March 1812

Their Majesties' Servants will present the favourite comedy of

The Wheel *of* Fortune

Sir David Daw	Mr GORDON	William	Mr HOWELL
Governor Tempest	Mr ROMER	Attendant	Mr TURNER
Sydenham	Mr DOBBS	Servants	Messrs. Wright,
Woodville	Mr ANDREWS	Woodward and D. Grant	
Henry Woodville	Mr CALDER	Emily Tempest	Mrs EDWIN
Weazel	Mr TAYLEUR	Mrs Woodville	Mrs WARD
Jenkins	Mr POWER	Dame Dunckley	Mrs TAYLEUR

Days of performing are:
Monday, Tuesday, Wednesday, Thursday and Friday.
Places with tickets to be taken of Mr Roberts at the box office of the theatre, from ten till three o'clock.

Boxes, 4s. 6d. —— Upper boxes, 4s. Pit 3s. —— Gallery, 1s.

The playbill for "The Wheel of Fortune" — it was most diverting.

Some pretty flowers my uncle bought me to wear at the theatre.

HUNSFORD PARSONAGE

Thursday 5th

Dear Diary,

I was extraordinarily sad to leave London! I am also not sure that I left Jane any happier.

However, here I am with Charlotte. We arrived at Hunsford in time for tea, after a journey that took us through fine, white-frosted country. Mr Collins welcomed us – repeatedly – to his humble abode and showed us every item of furniture! I think he wanted me to realize what I had lost by refusing him.

Charlotte seems content with her rather small, dark home. She tends not to listen to her husband, but encourages him to work outside in the garden. She seems to spend much of her time either in her parlour, paying parish visits or caring for her hens.

We are to have the dubious honour of seeing the esteemed Lady Catherine de Bourgh at church this Sunday. Oh la, I can hardly wait!

Mr C. is excessively proud of his topiary. Quite why I cannot tell.

Friday 6th

The whole household erupted in confusion today when Miss de Bourgh and her companion, Mrs Jenkinson, arrived at Hunsford gate. They did not deign to come into the house, but remained in their carriage, keeping poor Charlotte chatting outside in the cold.

Apparently we do not have to wait until Sunday to meet Lady Catherine, as we are summoned to dine at Rosings tomorrow. Mr Collins has congratulated us on our great good fortune more times than there are minutes in the day. Lord, his company is hard to bear!

Miss de Bourgh looks a perfect wife for Mr Darcy — sickly and cross!

ROSINGS Saturday 7th

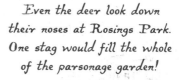

A beautiful spring day – there are even a few early lambs. It is a delight to escape into the fields for a walk and have some time to myself.

Now it nears the time for our visit to Rosings and I am hiding in my room. Mr C. is fussing about what we should wear and has already knocked on my door three times to implore me not to keep her ladyship waiting. I think poor Maria may pass out with nerves. Final call – we're off!

Even the deer look down their noses at Rosings Park. One stag would fill the whole of the parsonage garden!

LATER

Oh my dear Diary,

What an evening!

Lady Catherine was shockingly grand and shockingly tall. The house, furnishings, food and servants were all as fine as Mr Collins had foretold. It is not necessary to speak while at Rosings, as Lady Catherine delivers her opinion on every subject. She is so decisive that any controversy would be most unwelcome.

Her Ladyship could hardly believe that I had had no governess. For myself, I think that if Miss de Bourgh is the product of a governess, I have been well served – she said not a word all evening. She may be insipid, but she is at least a matching height for Mr Darcy!

La, what would Mr Collins say if he should read this? He already doubts my proper appreciation of the evening.

Nor would Jane approve of my unkindness!

MOTHER and DAUGHTER

Monday 9th

I was unable to write yesterday as we were much occupied by listening to Mr Collins' sermon in church, followed by Lady de Bourgh's sermon over tea. I fancy Sir William and Maria will be glad to return home. As for me, I am as happy here as anywhere – except London! I have found a pleasant walk along an open grove on the edge of Rosings. It is quiet and there are wild flowers in abundance. I counted fifteen varieties this afternoon.

I have managed to name all these wild flowers — Papa would be proud of me!

Thursday 12th

Sir William left for Meryton today and I think Maria longed to go with him! In the afternoon, Lady Catherine paid us the great honour of a visit. I suspect she comes merely to find fault with Charlotte's housekeeping or the arrangement of her furniture. Mr Collins greets every rude remark with boundless gratitude. It is my opinion that Charlotte would have done better to remain an old maid, but she does seem content. She loves her hens if not her husband! When it rains they jump into her arms for protection.

She has five different breeds.

Old English Game | Derbyshire Redcap | Norfolk Grey | Marsh Daisy | Rosecomb

I spend much of my time walking, writing to Jane or working on Papa's waistcoat!

Thursday 19th

Dear Diary,

I have been here for a fortnight and have been perfectly content. Now I hear that Mr Darcy and his cousin, Colonel Fitzwilliam, are to visit Rosings. I admit to a certain curiosity in seeing Mr Darcy and Miss de Bourgh together, but apart from that I wish Mr Darcy would refrain from disturbing the peace of the Kentish countryside. Lady Catherine talks of his arrival with the greatest satisfaction.

Tuesday 24th

Lord, what a fuss Mr Collins makes of each event. He was bustling about at cockcrow this morning, preparing to call upon Mr Darcy and Colonel Fitzwilliam. He later returned with the two gentlemen! Colonel Fitzwilliam is not particularly handsome, but he talks very pleasantly. Mr Darcy takes the usual view down his nose. When I enquired if he had seen Jane in London, knowing that he never had, he just mumbled. I fancy he looked a touch confused.

Colonel Fitzwilliam

Mr Collins was, of course, overcome by the honour of their visit. We ladies think that Colonel Fitzwilliam will add considerably to the pleasure of visits to Rosings – should we have the distinction of being invited again!

EASTER DAY

Sunday 29th

Just returned from church. Mr Collins must be responsible for hosts of heavenly angels tumbling off their clouds in boredom, for his sermon was both too long and too ponderous.

Now we are summoned to Rosings for supper. I will let you know later, dear Diary, how close Mr Darcy and Miss de Bourgh appear!

Meanwhile, I shall go and commune with the humble sheep of the fields. The country becomes greener and more lush every day. I shall take Charlotte's pugs with me and throw off Mr Collins' Sunday solemnity by chasing them down my favourite lane!

LATER

An altogether tiresome evening.

I can discern no symptom of love between Miss de Bourgh and Mr Darcy – it must certainly be an engagement of convenience. I could almost fancy that Mr Darcy paid more attention to me than Miss de Bourgh. Lady Catherine was outrageously rude about my piano playing. Only Colonel Fitzwilliam showed any charm or manners.

"Miss Bennet would not play at all amiss, if she practised more..."

Monday 30th

Oh Lord, I am quite discomposed! Charlotte and Maria went into the village earlier, while I stayed at the parsonage to write to Jane. Unfortunately, Mr Darcy came calling – just imagine my confusion! It was unimaginably awkward. Well, HE was most awkward. I hardly know how to describe his visit at all. He stood by the mantle, fidgeting from one foot to another – said hardly a word – then left as abruptly as he had arrived.

It is most unlike me not to be able to pin down a situation, yet I feel that Mr Darcy came with some intention that I missed altogether!

LATER

Charlotte, who as we know is lacking in all good sense, declares Mr Darcy must be in love with me – ha! After giving the matter some more thought, I suspect that he hoped to escape from Lady Catherine's company only to have the shock of falling into mine. Yet dear, foolish Charlotte advises me not to discount the advantages of marrying Mr Darcy, or, failing him, Colonel Fitwilliam. I feel it is time I returned home lest such madness is contagious!

APRIL

How can my life be so disagreeable when the countryside is at its most agreeable?

Thursday 9th

Dearest Diary,

I have been crying with frustration this last half hour. All have gone to take tea at Rosings, but I have remained behind for I am quite certainly indisposed.

While I was out walking this afternoon I ran into Colonel Fitzwilliam, who offered to escort me home. In the course of the conversation, he told me that Mr Darcy had lately saved his good friend, Mr Bingley, from "a most imprudent marriage." I could hardly contain myself. How could marrying my dear sister be considered imprudent?

All that Jane has suffered has been at Mr Darcy's hands. Oh, I had thought Miss Bingley to blame, but it was Mr Darcy's prejudice and arrogance. Fie upon his cruelty! He is the most hateful of men. My poor Jane. I shall comfort myself by re-reading all her letters.

PS – I could have grown to like Colonel Fitzwilliam, but now I do not feel disposed to regard any friends or relations of Mr Darcy's with favour.

MUCH LATER

It is late and I write this by the light of a single candle. I have yet more that I must recount, even though I am now so distressed that I can hardly hold my pen.

A crow-black night.

MY SECOND UNWELCOME PROPOSAL!

Caw-caw!

I had just started to read Jane's letters when a most unexpected visitor arrived – Mr Darcy! He appeared very agitated and he had every reason to be, for after much hesitation he declared that he loved me!

"In vain have I struggled.
It will not do. My feelings
will not be repressed.
You must allow me to
tell you how ardently
I admire and love you."

It is almost impossible to believe, but MR DARCY had come to propose marriage to me!

He made no effort to be charming or tender. Indeed, he seemed more concerned with my inferior family background, but he said that, in the end, his "love and admiration would not be repressed."

In spite of my deep dislike of the man, for a single second I felt sorry for him. Then I saw that smug look on his face – the surety that with my humble origins, I would not refuse such an offer. How my anger boiled! I told him instantly that I would never consider marrying a man who had injured my sister so, and had been the cause of all Mr Wickham's misfortunes.

MR DARCY SHOULD HAVE LEFT THEN – BUT HE DID NOT!

He stayed to accuse me of refusing him out of pride, because he had mentioned my inferior social background. Well, I felt no further need for politeness. I told him that his arrogance, conceit and selfish disdain of others had always convinced me that he would be the last man in the world that I would ever marry! He was clearly both astonished and mortified by this outburst and at last took his leave.

I too am astonished! That Mr Darcy should prevent Mr Bingley from marrying Jane and yet overcome the same reservations and propose marriage to me is most incredible. He may talk of my pride, but mine is entirely justified. His prejudice against my social background is abominable! As was his treatment of Mr Wickham. How could he believe I would marry him? How dare he make such an assumption!

The sun thought it might safely shine again — but it was wrong!

Friday 10th

My dearest Diary,

*I have in no way recovered my composure. Indeed, I have not – for I have yet **MORE** to relate. I was walking down my lane trying to calm myself after yesterday, when Mr Darcy again appeared most unexpectedly. Before I had a chance to object, he thrust a letter into my hands.*

Oh Diary, would that you had a voice! You might have pointed out the error of my judgement from the very beginning. I have put too much value on my ability to judge others. I have been blind, partial, ignorant and absurd.

If you wonder why I say these things, you only have to read this letter. I walked for hours reading it again and again and was unable to discount its truth.

Rosings
Thursday 9 April, 1812

Miss Elizabeth Bennet

Be not alarmed, Madam, this letter contains no renewal of the offer that was so disgusting to you. I know that you will read it unwillingly, but out of justice I would ask you to do so.

You accused me of two very different crimes last night. The first was of having detached Mr Bingley from your sister. This I admit. I realized on the evening of the dance at Netherfield that my friend's attachment to your sister was beyond anything I had witnessed before. I also realized that there was a general expectation of their marriage. But I could see no particular partiality on your sister's side, for she was charming and open to all.

Yet my objection to the marriage was more than that and more than your family connections. It pains me to offend you, but your mother's want of propriety and that of your three younger sisters led me to believe it would be a most unhappy connection for Mr Bingley.

Miss Bingley's uneasiness was equal to my own and so we acted together to persuade him of the evils of such a choice. I do not suppose we would have succeeded, had I not been able to convince him of your sister's indifference. I confess I did conceal from him that your sister has been staying in London. I did not knowingly wound your sister. I was trying to protect my friend.

Make haste, there's more!

Secondly, there is the more weighty accusation of my having destroyed Mr Wickham's prospects. This I can only refute. My father was his godfather and very fond of him. He paid for his education and hoped that Wickham would go into the church, and intended to provide a parish for him. Within half a year of my father's death Mr Wickham decided against the church, so I settled three thousand pounds on him. Three years later, the parish that had been intended for him became vacant and he wrote to say he would now like it. I, naturally, refused.

He was violent in his abuse of me, but later, he seemed resigned.

Then, last summer, a circumstance for which I must ask your secrecy presented itself.

My sister, who is ten years my junior, went to stay with her companion, Mrs Younge, in Ramsgate. Mrs Younge, in whose character we were unhappily deceived, knew Mr Wickham. With her connivance, he persuaded Georgiana, who was but fifteen, that she loved him and that they should elope. Luckily, she loved me as a father and was unable to deceive me. I arrived two days before the planned elopement and you can imagine how I felt and acted.

Mr Wickham's object was certainly my sister's fortune, but I suspect it was also a way of taking revenge on me. Colonel Fitzwilliam can verify the truth of this as he knows it all.

I will only add, God bless you.

Fitzwilliam Darcy

*What think you, my dear Diary?
Have I not reason to be humiliated and ashamed
of my conduct and that of my family?*

Till this moment I have never known myself. Even now I do not know what I think of Mr Darcy – except that he unsettles me. His manner has certainly been most ungentlemanly, yet it seems that I have wronged him, too. I was too easily deceived by Mr Wickham's outward appearance of good-natured honesty and Mr Darcy's disagreeable pride.

Hate him? Like him? Love him?

When I finally calmed myself enough to return to the parsonage, I learned that Mr Darcy and Colonel Fitzwilliam are to return to London. Perhaps it is for the best. I have no more to say on the matter.

Friday 17th

I have not written this last week – I have been too overwhelmed with shame at my lack of judgement. I cannot tell Charlotte what has passed, she would never understand. In truth, I do not understand. Mr Darcy is always in my thoughts, but quite why I do not know.

I long for the comfort of home and am relieved that Maria and I leave tomorrow. Papa wrote that he misses my company, and I miss his. Yet now I realize Jane lost her chance of happiness because of our family's lack of decorum, I do so wish that Papa would be firmer with Mama and my sisters. For myself, I am still mortified to have so misread Mr Wickham and others. Oh, Lizzy!

We have spent much time at Rosings the last few days. I amuse myself by imagining what Lady Catherine might have said if Mr Darcy had presented me as his future wife! There is little else to lift my spirits.

Saturday 18th

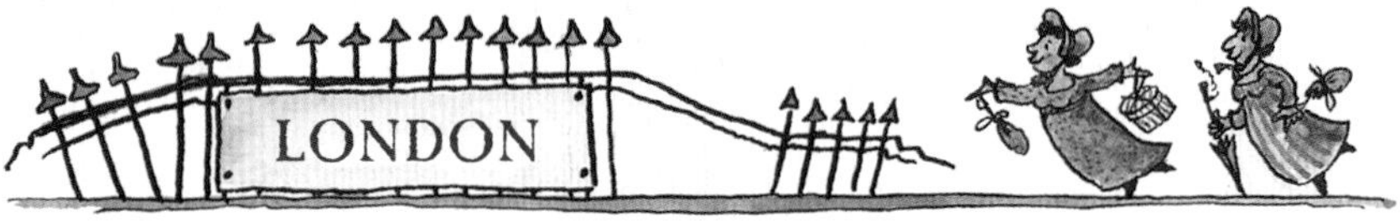

Maria and I left Hunsford after breakfast. Mr Collins' parting civilities were both humble and pompous – and lengthy. I could feel sorry for Charlotte, but her parish, poultry and pugs seem to meet her needs. Anyway, here we are in London at last!

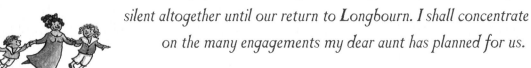

It is a joy to be with Jane and the Gardiners. I cannot yet decide how much of what has passed I should tell Jane. Certainly I shall have to wait, for we are hardly ever alone here and the bedroom walls are paper thin. So, my dear Diary, I think it best to keep silent altogether until our return to Longbourn. I shall concentrate on the many engagements my dear aunt has planned for us.

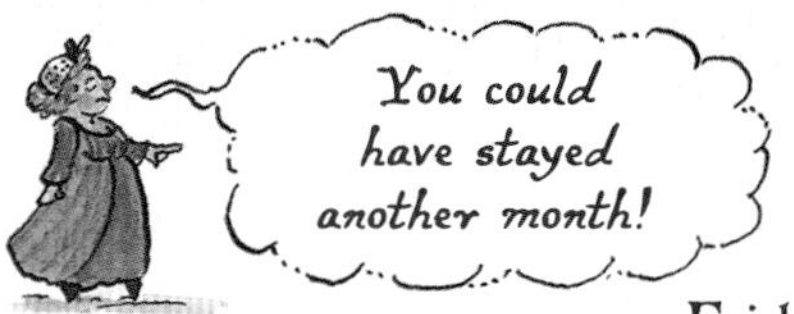

You could have stayed another month!

MAY

Oh, Lizzy, at last!

Friday 1st HOME AT LAST!

Mama is indifferent to my return, but Papa is delighted. Mary, Kitty and Lydia appear as silly as ever – only now I feel it even more than in the past. The regiment is soon to transfer to Brighton, and Lydia, Mama and Kitty all wish to spend the summer there. I trust Papa will not allow it.

Lydia talks of Mr Wickham a great deal. She revealed with delight that Miss King and her fortune would not have him! There was a time when I might have greeted this news with happiness. Now I suspect that Miss King may be a better judge of character than I have proved to be. I am glad she escaped. I have no wish to see Mr Wickham ever again and will avoid him if I can.

Saturday 2nd

I could wait no longer, and directly after breakfast I told Jane all about Mr Darcy's visit and his letter – all, that is, except about her and Mr Bingley. The whole tale sent my dear sister into confusion, for she could not make both Mr Darcy and Mr Wickham appear good. One has the goodness and the other the appearance of goodness!

We both felt it must have cost Mr Darcy dearly to relate the story of Mr Wickham and his beloved sister. We resolved not to expose Mr Wickham as a scoundrel for that might expose Miss Darcy's secret. Besides, who would believe us? There is such prejudice against Mr Darcy and such a liking for Wickham.

Thankfully, Mr Wickham will soon have quit Meryton for Brighton and that will end the matter.

It was a joy to walk again with Jane.

I felt so foolish when I first read Mr Darcy's letter – it is a relief to have Jane to comfort me. She was not surprised that I had caught the affection of Mr Darcy, loyal sister that she is. I wish I could tell her of Mr Bingley's warm feelings for her, but it would not change things and might bring her more pain.

<u>Friday 15th</u>

Such a beautiful day. Jane and I walked across the fields and picked a huge bunch of flowers and grasses. Now that I have had some time at home with Jane, I see how she pines for Mr Bingley. I fear she will always cherish him above all other men.

<u>Sunday 17th</u>

I shall never walk back home from church beside Mama again. She still harps on about the injustice done to Jane by Mr Bingley and appears comforted by the idea that Jane might die of a broken heart. Lord, she does vex me so! She wanted to know every detail of Charlotte's housekeeping and how often she referred to inheriting Longbourn.

Oh la, what is life without a redcoat?

<u>Saturday 23rd</u>

Jane and I have taken to bed with colds.

You do see, don't you, Miss Elizabeth?

Even as I lie in bed I can hear Lydia, Kitty and Mama lamenting the departure of the regiment. They lack all decorum and I cannot help seeing them through Mr Darcy's eyes. I can almost forgive him for wanting to protect his friend from such a family, but only almost! Jane scolds me, for I have ink on the sheets, oh dear!

Sunday 24th

It is not to be supported. Mrs Forster has invited Lydia to spend the summer in Brighton. Lydia flies about the house in raptures. Kitty is extremely peeved at not being invited. Jane and I have decided to stay in bed for another day!

Monday 25th

I spent a restless night thinking of what further damage might be caused by Lydia's imprudent manner in Brighton. After breakfast I left my bed to advise Papa not to let her go. However, he thinks only of his own peace, and fears he will have none if Lydia does not go. Papa can be impossible! Well, I have done my duty and can do no more. I just wish Lydia's expressions of excitement were not so voluble.

Friday is the regiment's last night in Meryton and some of the officers are to dine with us. I fear Mr Wickham is among the party and I am not disposed to enjoy his company. I wish my cold would return.

Friday 29th

A most painful evening. Mr Wickham tried to single me out as before, but I rebuffed him at every turn. I told him that I had seen Mr Darcy in Kent and felt that he improved on proper acquaintance, which is the truth!

Mr Wickham looked most uncomfortable and tried to return to the subject of his old grievances. I was in no humour to indulge him on this subject and I believe he soon got the message. I think I can say that we parted with a mutual desire never to meet again! Lydia went home with the Forsters, for they leave for Brighton early tomorrow. Kitty is in her room, howling!

JUNE

Monday 1st

Whilst I am delighted that Mr Wickham has removed to Brighton, I am less happy that the rest of the regiment has also gone. There is no socializing to look forward to and Mama and Kitty are impossible. I am still working on Papa's waistcoat, but may tear it to shreds if they don't stop moaning on about visiting Brighton.

Only the thought of journeying to the Lakes stops me from being a complete grump. I wish Jane was coming too, but she is to be left in charge of our little cousins. They do adore her and may lift her spirits, for Mama, Kitty and Mary will certainly not.

I feel I should be honest with you, my dear Diary – Mr Darcy remains in my thoughts, but I still cannot tell you why.

The poet Mr Wordsworth lives in the Lake District. He who wrote:

"My heart leaps up when I behold
A rainbow in the sky."

As does mine! It would be delightful to meet him.

William Wordsworth

Monday 8th

Another week has passed with little to mark it. Lydia sent two letters to Kitty, but from what I could see they were too full of underlining to be made public. At least Kitty may come to her senses without the regiment or her sister to lead her on.

I shall try to return from the Lakes with greater patience for my family and less eagerness to judge others – especially when not in possession of all the facts.

Fie, Lizzy, you had best not curb your sharp observations entirely or you will have nothing to write about!

Thursday 11th

Oh la, Lizzy is most put out!

I am most disappointed – I have just received the news that we are not to go to the Lakes after all. Our trip has been delayed until July, we will only have three weeks away and we are only going as far as Derbyshire. Oh Lord, I hope I may enter Derbyshire without meeting Mr Darcy. I had far rather go to the Lakes and meet Mr Wordsworth!

Lydia is sixteen this week. I doubt that it will make her more sensible!

Friday 12th

Dearest Diary,

Forgive me, Jane is so out of sorts and my other sisters so trying I think it best if I take a short break. I only write to moan, which is neither entertaining for you nor good for me. I could write about Cook letting the cats eat the venison or Hill breaking Papa's inkwell, but would you really wish to know?

Oh my, oh my!

I will say goodbye for now, but will renew our acquaintance once I have left for Derbyshire. I shall then be able to entertain you with a traveller's tale or two. La, I can hardly wait!

I believe Derbyshire has many hills and forests — I fancy I shall like it!

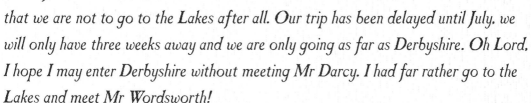

AUGUST

Sunday 2nd

ON TOUR AT LAST!

Dearest Diary,

I am so enraptured by travel! As each day passes my routine worries seem a little less important and a little more absurd. My aunt and uncle are delightful company and we have travelled through miles of beautiful countryside.

Apart from missing Jane, all is quite perfect. We have now reached Derbyshire and the little town of Lambton, where we are to spend a few days in this charming inn.

Our route took us beside the River Wye.

My aunt used to live locally and wishes to renew old acquaintances, so I have leisure to write.

She tells me that Pemberley is only five miles from here. I hope she doesn't take it into her head to visit, for I should be mortified to come across Mr Darcy – he might think I was seeking another marriage proposal!

Monday 3rd

I woke before the morning chorus. I was too nervous to write of it last night, but my aunt intends to visit Pemberley today! The chambermaid promises that the family are not at home, but I still feel unsettled. More of this later. I am going for a walk to calm myself, for I must not let my aunt know that I am flustered.

I do hope the chambermaid is not mistaken.

Tuesday 4th

I can hardly think. Oh, how my hand shakes. How confused are my thoughts. I must calm myself, but I know not how. I wish to write, and yet where to start? Oh, Lizzy, just get on with it!

Well, Pemberley is surely the most beautiful estate. The house is utterly charming, and is so full of treasures that parts of it are open to the public. The housekeeper gave us a tour and showed us the portraits of Mr Darcy and his family. There was even one of Mr Wickham. Apparently, he left many debts in the Shire, all paid by Mr Darcy! She spoke very warmly of Mr Darcy, but had not a good word for Mr Wickham.

After we had seen the house we took a walk around the grounds. As I paused to look upon the magnificent house I might have lived in, I saw Mr Darcy coming down the drive! I could not avoid his eyes, but I was overcome with agitation and feel sure I blushed. I could not bear him to think I had come to throw myself in his path again.

Why, Miss Elizabeth, what an unexpected surprise.

He is even more pleasing than Mr Wordsworth!

I tried to make it plain that we thought he was arriving on the morrow and he agreed that had been his plan. I was not myself at all, but he was charming and open – quite different from his former self. He even invited my uncle to fish on the estate, and did not look down his nose once!

Please turn over in haste — for there is more!

His sister arrives tomorrow and he wishes us to meet! Can you believe it? He cannot think too ill of me for this is a great compliment. My aunt and uncle are very taken by him and cannot understand his reputation for pride and vanity. My aunt even ventured that he was near as handsome as Mr Wickham!

Afterwards, we went on to visit some friends of my aunt, but I hardly know what they look like for I was entirely taken up with thinking of Mr Darcy and Pemberley. Mr Darcy was so civil and to think he wishes me to meet his sister! They are to call the day after tomorrow – I shall stay close to the inn so as not to miss them. How could I have judged Mr Darcy so harshly?

This is how I remember my first view of Pemberley. Although to be sure it is all far more handsome than I can portray.

Wednesday 5th

Oh, I am amazed at myself and my discomposure! Mr Darcy just called upon us with his sister and Mr Bingley! I had not expected them until tomorrow and had not expected Mr Bingley at all. I knew not what to think and I know my aunt and uncle were most surprised by the honour.

Miss Darcy was wearing a charming hat and gown that her brother had acquired from Paris. It had long sleeves!

Georgiana

I am up!

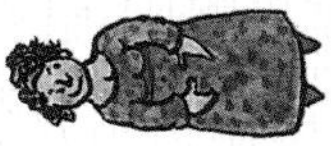

I am down!

I spin!

Mr Darcy's sister, Georgiana, is not in the least proud. She is a little shy but quite charming, and she has a sweet, good-humoured face. Mr Bingley remembered to the day when we last met, 26 November, at the Netherfield Ball. Surely such exactness must mean that he still treasures the memory of dancing with Jane?

Mr Darcy was as affable as he had been yesterday. A few weeks ago he would hardly have deigned to talk to my aunt and uncle, but now he is so free of self-consequence, so open and desirous to please. He has invited us to dine at Pemberley on Friday! Mr Bingley expressed his delight at this and his desire to hear more about his Hertfordshire friends. He must mean Jane...

LATER

I have been lying in bed these last two hours, quite unable to sleep. I keep thinking of Mr Darcy. It is certain that I no longer hate him, but I cannot say with any certainty what my emotions might be.

I can admit to being discomposed by him. I am also charmed by his forgiving nature, for he seems to hold no grudge against me for my rude rejection. Can he still love me? He seems to solicit not only my good opinion, but that of my aunt and uncle.

I cannot think!

I stand!

Should I love him? Could I love him? Do I love him?
All that is certain is that he keeps me from my sleep!
Fie on you, Mr Darcy!

I cannot eat!

So, is this love?

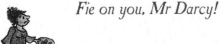

<u>Thursday 6th</u>

In haste, as my uncle is to fish with the gentlemen at Pemberley this morning, while my aunt and I return Georgiana's call. I am all of a dither. I think I would quite like it if Mr Darcy chose not to fish!

LATER

Our visit started with many awkward silences, for Miss Bingley and Mrs Hurst were there as well as Miss Darcy. The sisters hardly acknowledged my aunt and Miss Darcy was too shy to speak. Luckily Mr Darcy left his fishing rod and came to rescue the conversation – but I felt my aunt's eyes upon me every time he addressed me.

To my mind, there is only one reason for a gentleman to pay a lady so much attention!

It is plain that Miss Bingley has not given up her designs on Mr Darcy and it is equally clear that he has no interest in her. She tried to embarrass me by alluding to Mr Wickham. I saw poor Georgiana turn ghostly white. Miss Bingley cannot know how any mention of that gentlemen must upset Georgiana and Mr Darcy. I answered her with great coolness and she did not pursue the subject.

My aunt and I did not talk of Mr Darcy as we returned in the carriage. I fancy she would have liked to and I am not entirely disinterested in the subject!

I am not sure what I expected from the visit, but I feel vaguely dissatisfied.

I look forward to dinner at Pemberley tomorrow.
Indeed I do!

Friday 7th

TERRIBLE NEWS!

I found this pheasant's feather on the drive of Pemberly. It was only yesterday, but seems so long ago.

Dearest Diary,

It is late and I am exhausted by emotion and travel, yet I am too anxious for sleep. Lydia has eloped with Mr Wickham! We are staying at an inn on the road back to Longbourn. We set out this morning soon after the arrival of this letter from Jane.

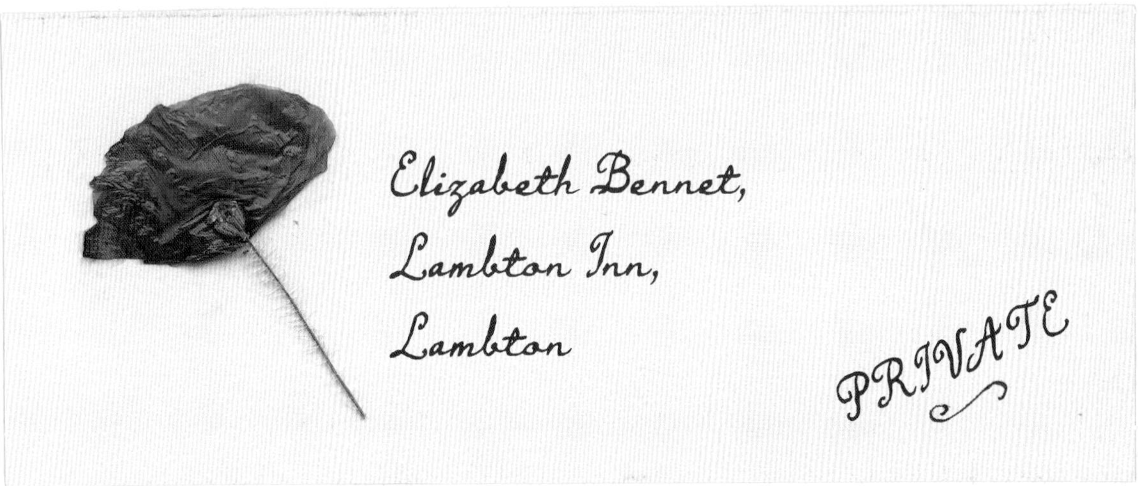

Mr Darcy arrived just as I had read the letter. I was so overcome with emotion that I could not hide my shock, and told him all. He was much concerned and very kind. But this will end our acquaintance for certain – and I find I mind that most painfully. Oh, I surely do. Yet I cannot dwell on that now.

I fear there is little hope of Lydia and Wickham being married, for Lydia has no fortune to offer Wickham. I never even thought that Lydia favoured him, but I suspect she would favour any man who paid her attention. If only I had told my family what I knew of Wickham's true nature, I might have prevented this elopement.

A crow-black day.

I wish the morning would come so that we could be on the road again. I ache to be at Longbourn and close to Jane. Lydia has thrown our family into the deepest disgrace and Jane and I have lost all chance of happiness. I cannot but blame myself for not disclosing Wickham's true worth. What a fool I have been!

LONGBOURN

Dear Hill greeted us with steaming mugs of hot milk and honey.

Saturday 8th

Quite exhausted, but home at last.

Papa has written that he can find no trace of Lydia and Wickham in London. Mama has taken to her room. Jane is as pale as death. But Kitty knew of Lydia's plan all along! As for Mary, she delights in declaring that "the loss of virtue in a female is irretrievable – one false step involves her in endless ruin." Thank you, Mary – it involves her sisters in endless ruin, too.

It seems that Denny has told Colonel Forster that Wickham will never marry Lydia, which is as I thought. Colonel Forster has given Jane the note that Lydia wrote to his wife before her elopement. Oh, the thoughtless, thoughtless creature! At least she seemed to think they would get married.

My dear Harriet,

You will laugh when you know where I am gone, and I cannot help laughing myself at your surprise. I am going to Gretna Green, and if you cannot guess with whom, I shall think you a simpleton. You need not send them word at Longbourn of my going, for it will make the surprise the greater, when I write to them and sign my name Lydia Wickham. What a good joke that will be!

Your affectionate friend, Lydia Bennet

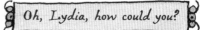

Oh, Lydia, how could you?

Have you heard?
Of course, I have given my condolences.
I blame her Papa.
Now, don't tell a soul!

My poor Papa, how he will feel this. Yet it is Jane I worry most for. She does not look well and has shouldered every care and anxiety herself. Lady Lucas knows of Lydia's elopement and has been to offer her condolences. I wish she had stayed at home and triumphed over us at a distance. Soon the whole Shire will know.

Now, now Mrs Bennet, all will be well.

Sunday 9th

Mr Gardiner has left to join Papa in London. My dear aunt and cousins are to remain with us for a few days, which is a great comfort. Mrs Gardiner is wonderful with Mama and endeavours to keep our spirits up.

Monday 10th

No letters, no news. A day of misery and anxiety.

Tuesday 11th

A letter from my uncle. He and Papa have found no sign of Wickham and Lydia. He asks if I know of any family that Wickham might have, but I know of none.

Dear Mrs Gardiner continues to raise our spirits, unlike my other aunt, Mrs Philips. She pays us daily visits, always with some new report of Mr Wickham's misdeeds.

Such debts.
Such flirting.
Such gambling.
So many broken promises!
Our very dear aunt, Mrs Philips!

Wednesday 12th

The arrival of the post is all we have to look forward to. Every morning we hope that some good news will arrive. Jane has Papa's instructions to open all his letters, but so far there has been no news to cheer us. Today this arrived – it is hard to believe that the sender of this letter is related to us.

Mr Bennet,
Longbourn, near Meryton

To think that Charlotte is married to him and that she was once my best friend. He must be greatly relieved that I refused him! We do our best to keep Mama calm, but it is hard when such letters arrive. Dear Jane looks paler every day.

Friday 14th

My aunt has received a letter from Mr Gardiner. Wickham and Lydia are still not found and Wickham has left large gaming debts in Brighton.

Mr Gardiner has prevailed upon Papa to come home tomorrow, so my aunt has decided to return to London. We will all miss her and my little cousins. At least they are always merry.

Today my cousins hid Mary's music in the shrubbery!

I can share this with none but you, my dear Diary, but if I had not recently come to feel so warmly towards Mr Darcy, I could have born Lydia's infamy better. Now the knowledge of all that is lost torments me, and my nights seem very long. I am utterly devastated.

Saturday 15th

Mrs Gardiner left early this morning and Papa is now returned. He blames himself and although he appears his usual philosophical self, I believe he is much chastened and will not be allowing his other daughters such freedom.

Monday 17th

Oh, such a day, I cannot say what my feelings are. This letter from my dear, dear uncle came by express from London.

My father has already written his agreement. Yet he believes my uncle must have given Wickham at least ten thousand pounds to persuade him to marry Lydia. My dear, generous uncle. How is even half this sum ever to be repaid? Papa has never been one to make savings.

My foolish mother has gone from alarm and vexation to transports of delight. She has already dressed and gone off to Meryton to spread the good news. Her favourite daughter married at sixteen! Jane tried to temper her happiness by reminding her what we must owe to Mr Gardiner, but she thinks only of herself and Lydia.

I am hiding in my room for I am truly sick of my mother's folly. Although I must be thankful for this outcome, I can see no cause to rejoice in it, for with such a husband Lydia's misery is certain. Jane thinks that Wickham cannot be so bad after all. She is too good to have proper sense.

Tuesday 18th

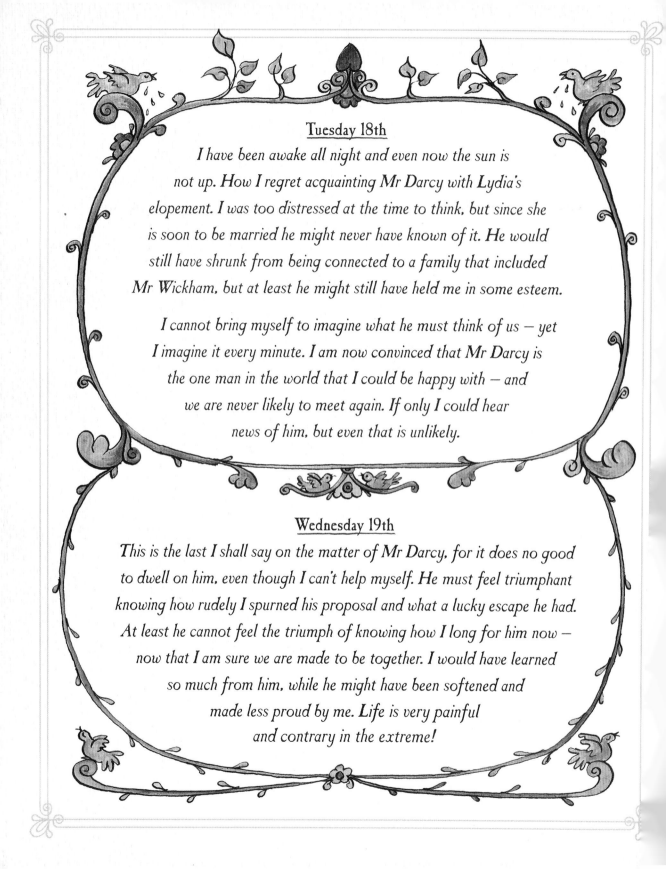

I have been awake all night and even now the sun is not up. How I regret acquainting Mr Darcy with Lydia's elopement. I was too distressed at the time to think, but since she is soon to be married he might never have known of it. He would still have shrunk from being connected to a family that included Mr Wickham, but at least he might still have held me in some esteem.

I cannot bring myself to imagine what he must think of us – yet I imagine it every minute. I am now convinced that Mr Darcy is the one man in the world that I could be happy with – and we are never likely to meet again. If only I could hear news of him, but even that is unlikely.

Wednesday 19th

This is the last I shall say on the matter of Mr Darcy, for it does no good to dwell on him, even though I can't help myself. He must feel triumphant knowing how rudely I spurned his proposal and what a lucky escape he had. At least he cannot feel the triumph of knowing how I long for him now – now that I am sure we are made to be together. I would have learned so much from him, while he might have been softened and made less proud by me. Life is very painful and contrary in the extreme!

Thursday 20th

Papa has had another letter from my uncle. He has paid all Mr Wickham's debts in Brighton and urges Papa to do the same in Meryton. The wedding is to take place on Monday week and then Lydia and Mr Wickham are to go North, where Wickham is to become a regular soldier. Lydia wishes to visit Longbourn on the way and Jane and I persuaded Papa to allow this. He was most unwilling to acknowledge her or Wickham.

Saturday 22nd

Dearest Diary,

I am going to stop writing until Lydia and Wickham's visit is over. I feel overrun by a contradiction of feelings, both with regard to Lydia and to Mr Darcy. Oh, I know, I've mentioned his name AGAIN.

I am also exceedingly concerned for Jane. She has not mentioned Mr Bingley once and would not thank me for doing so, but I am sure he exercises her mind as much as Mr Darcy does mine. Just to write Mr Darcy's name comforts me.

I will confess it now: this rose petal that has been hiding in your pages is from Pemberley.

LYDIA'S WEDDING DAY

A day of relief,
but not celebration!

Monday 31st

I know I said that I would stop writing, but how else can I preserve my countenance? I regret now that I ever persuaded Papa to allow Lydia and Wickham to stay here. The married couple arrived late this afternoon and after an hour in their company I fled from the room. Lydia is quite unabashed and Wickham behaves as though he is a welcome new member of the family. Even Jane blushed for them. We none of us enquired how the wedding had gone, for it is a subject best not mentioned. Besides, it must have been a paltry affair with no guests or wedding feast.

Oh la, Mama,
greet your married daughter!

Mrs Bennet,
greet your divine son-in-law!

Oh my, oh my,
was ever a mother so blessed?

I must go down for dinner, but I would far rather starve in my room.

You may wish to starve,
but I require my titbits.

LATER

Are we really to tolerate ten days of this? At dinner Lydia took Jane's place on Mama's right. She told Jane that she must move lower since she is not yet married. I despair of Papa – how could he allow it? What is more, Mr Wickham shows no affection for Lydia, whilst she flirts with him. It is intolerable.

SEPTEMBER

Writing and drawing help me to order my thoughts, but sometimes they just won't be ordered!

A STRANGE REVELATION

<u>Wednesday 2nd</u>

Dearest Diary,

Lydia insisted on recounting the events of her wedding to Jane and me today. We both expressed a desire not to discuss the matter, but Lydia has no shame. Well, for once I was glad she hasn't, for although the wedding was certainly a sad little event, with my uncle giving Lydia away and my aunt being most severe, Lydia let slip an extraordinary snippet:

Mr Darcy attended the ceremony!

Oh my good Lord, what can this mean? Lydia clapped her hand over her mouth after mentioning Mr Darcy, for she had sworn not to tell anyone that he had been there. I was burning to press her on the subject, but Jane declared that if it was a secret we would ask no more.

You can imagine my turmoil of thought. I cannot let the matter rest and must discover why Mr Darcy attended Lydia's wedding. I will have to write to my aunt, yet I know I should not and Jane would be shocked.

Oh, a pox on goodness, it is a most annoying habit!

LATER

Too late for regrets! I have dispatched a note to my aunt. One way or another, I will discover why Mr Darcy was at Lydia's wedding.

Forget-me-nots!

Tuesday 8th

It is not to be borne, I cannot hear myself sing!

Dearest Diary,

Imagine my excitement when I saw that there was a letter from my dear, dear aunt. I ran to the shrubbery to be alone, for I could tell from the length that she had written all she knew, and my heart beat louder than the bird song.

From: Mrs Gardiner,
Gracechurch Street,
London

Elizabeth Bennet,
Longbourn

Oh, oh, oh, what to think! My heart whispers that Mr Darcy may have done all this for me. Yet it cannot be so, for I refused him so rudely and am now the sister-in-law of Wickham. We owe everything to Mr Darcy – he has restored Lydia's character and the reputation of our family.

I am so ashamed of myself and all that I have said and thought of him in the past. His compassion overwhelms his pride. I wish my aunt were right and that he still held affectionate feelings towards me, but I am now too humble to believe it.

How many daisies before he loves me?

And yet ... and yet. Oh, I would that it were so.

Wednesday 9th

Is not my husband quite charming?

Jane and I are of one mind – we cannot wait for Wickham and Lydia's departure tomorrow. Lydia is insensible to the pain she has caused and Wickham is only to be tolerated for her sake.

I read my aunt's letter at least once every hour and the part where she says she likes Mr Darcy at least twice every hour! I have not shared it with Jane yet, but I will.

Thursday 10th

Lydia and Wickham have gone! Lydia didn't appear to care one jot about leaving us and Wickham behaved as though he were the finest husband in the Shire. Mama is in a decline at the loss of her favourite daughter. Papa is relieved.

I have been thinking long about Mr Darcy. I feel he may still like me – just a little!

Wednesday 16th

Dearest Diary,

I have not written this last week for I, and the rest of Longbourn, have been in a strange humour since Lydia's departure. Well, that is about to change, for my Aunt Philips has just paid us a call.

As usual Mrs Philips brings all the gossip, and what gossip she brought today: Mr Bingley is to return to Netherfield! Jane colours every time it is mentioned and you may imagine that Mama mentions it most often!

Jane says she only colours as she fears what everyone must say, not because she has any feelings for Mr Bingley. I feel sure Mr Bingley is still fond of Jane. Yet I will leave the matter there as the poor man should not have to suffer this speculation. Mama will address the matter for all of us!

Once more my bonnet may go flying!

Thursday 17th

It must be a year since Mr Bingley first arrived at Netherfield and Mama nagged Papa to call upon him. Well, now she repeats herself and so does Papa, for he is again refusing to call on Mr Bingley.

I'm fine.
Sort of fine.
Really fine.
Mr Bingley is fine.

Poor Jane, I have never seen her so disturbed. It might have been better for us all if the whole of last year had not happened, yet think of the dullness! Still, my novel might have been written and Papa's waistcoat completed!

I'm fine.
Almost fine.

Friday 18th

Dearest, dearest Diary,

Never let me talk of Mr Darcy again; do not listen; do not permit it. The gentleman is banned from my thoughts. He and Mr Bingley called on us today and left me feeling most wretched. Both gentlemen seemed ill at ease, even Mr Bingley, although I could see Jane's beauty was working its old magic on him.

Mama was most ungracious and kept boasting of Lydia and Wickham's marriage! She may not know what she owes Mr Darcy in this matter, but her continued rudeness pains me terribly. I found myself unable to make any effort at normal conversation.

I kept my eyes on Papa's waistcoat, but I swear I shall have to undo every stitch my shaking hand embroidered. Why, if Darcy came to be silent and indifferent, did he come at all?

Does he no longer care for me? Oh, teasing, teasing man! I will not think of him.

Mrs Bennet has engaged them both to dine at Longbourn on Tuesday. I think I shall be indisposed. No, I would not miss it for all the ducks on Pemberley Lake!

LATER

Jane tells me she is delighted that Mr Bingley is to dine with us, for then all will see that they are now indifferent acquaintances. I cannot but laugh, for I think she is in very grave danger of making him as much in love with her as ever.

Life, how vexatious you are!

<u>Monday 21st</u>

Jane and I went for a walk to get away from Mama's preparations for tomorrow's dinner. We did not walk towards Netherfield! The country is looking particularly beautiful, for the leaves are on the turn, but not yet fallen. The autumn sun shone kindly and whilst my mood is somewhat fretful, a light has returned to Jane's eyes.

I am keeping these autumn leaves.
I fancy they match the colour
of a certain gentleman's eyes.

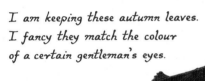

<u>Tuesday 22nd</u>

THE DINNER

Well, that was not a pleasant occasion. We were a large party, but the only guests I cared about were Mr Bingley and Mr Darcy. At dinner, Mr Bingley took his old place next to Jane. Mr Darcy was next to Mama, which could not have been worse or further away from me. Then we were sat at different tables for cards and I didn't once see him glance my way. Mama invited them to stay on after cards, but their carriage was already waiting.

Jane imagines that Mr Bingley never had any design of engaging her affection and is just charming to all! She is not to be teased on the matter and will not permit me even to smile at my own thoughts! My thoughts of Mr Darcy do not make me smile.

Thursday 24th

Mr Bingley called on us this morning! Mr Darcy has returned to London for a few days, so Mr Bingley came alone. He was in remarkably good humour and is to dine with us tomorrow. I do not, will not, have not smiled at Jane. Lord no, I do not even raise an eyebrow!

Miss Bennet, so delightful...!

I am not sorry that Mr Darcy has returned to London for he was doing no good here.

Friday 25th

Dearest Diary,

I am still refraining from all comments. Indeed, I hardly dare breathe lest everything goes wrong again. However, Mr Bingley arrived for dinner very promptly – he came in the morning, before we were even dressed!

But nothing is cooked yet!

Lizzy, come away!

Mama spent the rest of the morning contriving to leave him and Jane alone, but Jane would not have it and I remained with her at all times. Bingley bore it all with noble good humour and was in every way charming. He comes tomorrow morning to shoot with Papa.

Jane has not mentioned any indifference to Mr Bingley this evening. I hardly dare look at her for smiling. I will not cloud her happiness by thinking of Mr Darcy – for this evening at least.

Papa's pheasants have little to look forward to.

AN ENGAGEMENT!

♥♥♥

Saturday 26th

Dearest, dearest Diary,

Happiness and delight is all ours – Jane is engaged to Mr Bingley! Even Papa is pleased.

Papa went shooting with Mr Bingley in the morning. When they returned Mama finally contrived to leave the pair alone and the next thing I knew was that they were engaged! Dear Jane wonders how she will bear such happiness, but I suspect she will.

It is a wonder to me that an affair that has caused so much vexation has now been arranged with such rapidity. Lydia is forgotten and Mama's new favourite is Jane. Mary can't wait to use the library at Netherfield and Kitty dreams of endless balls. Everyone is happy.

<u>Sunday 27th</u>

My dear Diary,

I suspect that you and I will soon become even closer companions, for Jane now speaks only to Mr Bingley. She does seek me out if he is occupied, but only to discuss the wonder of their happiness. He does the same if Jane is occupied, so I do still have my uses.

I know that Jane wishes that I too could find such happiness, but I fear it was mine to take and I let it pass me by. Maybe, if I am very lucky, another Mr Collins may ride my way! No – still I would not have him!

Imagine, two daughters married — and so well!

I suspect that Mama has told her sister, Mrs Philips, of the engagement, for I saw them whispering in church. Within a day the whole of Meryton will be talking of it!

<u>Tuesday 29th</u> AT LAST!

Today I finished embroidering Papa's waistcoat! I have only to sew it together and add the buttons. I walked into Meryton with Mary and Kitty to buy the thread. I think that in the future I may be in their company more than I might wish.

Here come the three old Bennet maids!

I will not count the months this has taken.

Saturday 3rd

OCTOBER

I am not to be trifled with.

My dearest Diary,

Oh my goodness gracious! I am in a confusion of surprise, amazement, shock and anger. Lady Catherine de Bourgh has just called on me. She travelled all the way from Rosings expressly to forbid me to marry Mr Darcy! You think it cannot be true? I know it cannot be true and yet it is.

It must be a falsehood.

I insist on being satisfied.

Do you know who I am?

Mr Collins had told Lady Catherine of Jane's engagement to Mr Bingley. Somehow this led her to believe that I should soon be engaged to Mr Darcy. She would not insult her nephew by supposing there was any truth in this, yet she wished to make it clear that she forbade it!

You will be despised.

Lady Catherine said that it was her dearest wish that Mr Darcy should marry her daughter. Two noble, respectable, honourable families joined in matrimony. I could not have been angrier or more insulted. I finally admitted that I was not engaged to her nephew, but when she asked me to promise never to enter into such an engagement, I refused. We had been walking in the shrubbery and her insults followed me as I ran back to the house. I did not invite her in and she took no leave of me.

Is Pemberley to be polluted?

Luckily, Mama thinks she called to bring news of Charlotte, and Jane has her mind elsewhere, so I have not been closely questioned.

Sunday 4th

I have been thinking more of Lady Catherine's visit. As I turn it over in my mind it seems even more unlikely now that Mr Darcy might choose me over his dignity. If he is at all fond of his aunt she may sway his purpose. Oh, I know not, but if he does not return to Netherfield soon, I shall guess that Lady Catherine has prevailed upon his pride.

If this is the case, I shall soon cease to regret him, for he will not be the gentleman I imagine him to be.

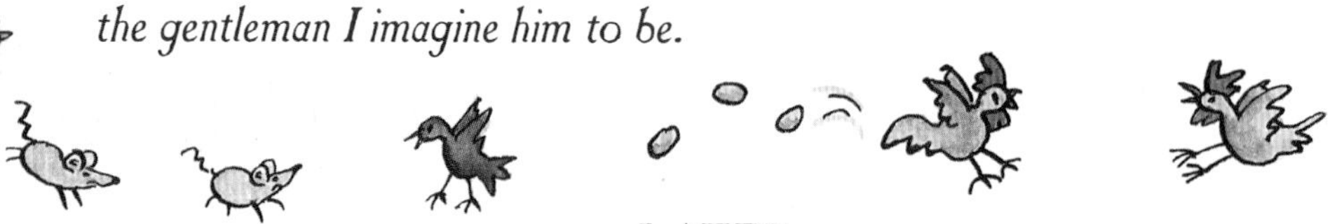

LATER

Papa called me into his study. He has had another unpleasant letter from Mr Collins. This time he warned Papa not to permit my engagement to Mr Darcy, as his esteemed patron, Lady Catherine, does not look on the match with friendly eyes.

Papa thought this a great joke and utterly absurd, since everyone knows how much I dislike that gentleman. It is also well known hereabouts that Mr Darcy disdains our country society. I was forced to laugh with Papa, when really I wanted to run away and cry. How can Papa, who sees so much, not have noticed that Mr Darcy did not look upon me with disdain? Or have I fancied too much?

The pigs got loose in the yard today.

Monday 5th

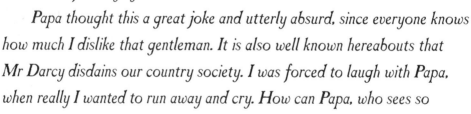

Jane with Bingley all day! I have one button left to sew on Papa's waistcoat. I am saving it for tomorrow. Mr Darcy has not returned to Netherfield.

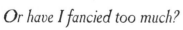

Tuesday 6th

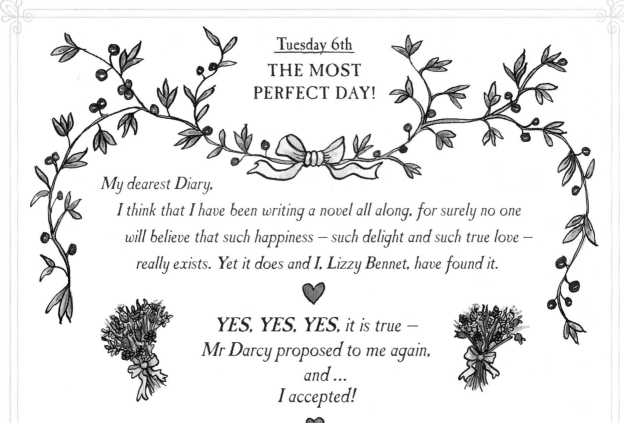

THE MOST PERFECT DAY!

My dearest Diary,

I think that I have been writing a novel all along, for surely no one will believe that such happiness – such delight and such true love – really exists. Yet it does and I, Lizzy Bennet, have found it.

***YES, YES, YES,** it is true –*
Mr Darcy proposed to me again,
and ...
I accepted!

I must pinch myself to believe that I exist in such a whirl of emotion. How I love the lanes hereabout, for it all happened when Mr Darcy and I were walking along them today. If you want me to start at the beginning you will be disappointed, for I will start with his declaration of love.

He called me his
"Dearest, loveliest, Elizabeth"!

*And much else besides, which I shall keep close to my heart. Yet his words were so heartfelt and received by me with such joy that with each one we drew closer and closer together. Well, I will tell you one other thing – he said that within half an hour of my visit to Pemberley he had known that his heart was **STILL MINE!***

THIS IS HOW IT HAPPENED:

Mr Darcy had arrived early with Mr Bingley and I was sent to walk with him so that Jane and Mr Bingley might be alone. I took this opportunity of thanking Mr Darcy for all he had done for Lydia. He was shocked that I had learned of it, but declared that he had done it for me, not for my family – just with thoughts of me.

He said that he had had a visit from his aunt, Lady Catherine. She had sought to turn him against me by repeating all that I had recently said to her. Far from putting Mr Darcy off, it gave him hope. He knew that if I had no feelings for him I should not have hesitated to say so. Then he said that his affections and wishes were unchanged and asked if I might now "consider doing him the honour of becoming his wife."

He holds no grudge for my past refusal of him, but believes I was entirely justified in my rebuke and said that he had been properly humbled by me.

Again and again he called me his "dearest, loveliest Elizabeth". He even quoted some of my favourite verses from the poet George Gordon Byron! Is he not quite perfect?

She walks in beauty, like the night
Of cloudless climes and starry skies;
And all that's best of dark and bright
Meet in her aspect and her eyes;
Thus mellowed to that tender light
Which heaven to gaudy day denies.

I could not feel my feet upon the ground.
I love you Mr Darcy! I wonder how long I have loved you without knowing.

Wednesday 7th

BEFORE DAWN!

Jane and I were up half the night talking. She could not believe that I love Mr Darcy and thought our engagement must be a joke. I explained that my love for him came upon me so gradually that I hardly knew it myself – but that he is now the only gentleman I would ever consider marrying! I also had to tell her that it was Mr Darcy who had saved Lydia.

Now I am all nerves, for Mr Darcy will come today to ask Papa's permission. How will I convince Papa that I truly love the man I have always professed to detest? Then there is Mama. She hates Mr Darcy beyond all others. I wish I had been more moderate in my expressions of distaste!

LATER

It was just as I thought! Papa gave Mr Darcy his permission, but could not readily believe I truly wished to marry him. He knows I would be unhappy if I did not marry for love. Poor Papa, it is no wonder he was confused, but eventually I convinced him.

I had to tell him of Mr Darcy's part in Lydia's marriage, which I think relieved his mind. He has worried about how to repay Mr Gardiner, but will not worry so much about repaying his son-in-law. Oh, my dear Papa! He shall wear his waistcoat to our wedding. Oh la, "our wedding" – I cannot believe it!

I told Mama of our engagement just before we retired for bed. She sat for a long while without saying a word. Then she jumped up and down in a flurry of ecstasy. She had quite forgotten her dislike of Mr Darcy. A house in town and ten thousand a year made him the most charming gentleman in all of England.

Ten thousand a year and very likely more!

I am now Mama's "sweetest Lizzy"!

Oh, Mr Darcy ... it is all too fresh in my mind for me to feel quite easy with it, but I fancy I shall wake tomorrow with a heart that bursts for the joy of all that lies before me!

Thursday 8th

Oh happiness, you are my friend indeed! Mr Darcy and Mr Bingley dined with us and Mr Darcy is in every way quite the most charming gentleman to be engaged to.

He declares that he was in the middle of loving me before he knew it. He calls my every impertinence "liveliness of mind"! He sits beside me now writing to Lady Catherine of our engagement. How she will bear the pollution of her family by Lizzy Bennet can be well imagined!

It is time I replied to my dear aunt's letter, for until now I have been unable to answer her hints of Mr Darcy's attachment. Now she may indulge her imagination as much as she chooses for it will all be true! I shall send her Mr Darcy's warmest love and say he insists they come to Pemberley for Christmas. There she may take a turn around the grounds in an open carriage, if she promises not to catch cold.

Mr Darcy says that I may have two ponies as a wedding gift!

My little cousins and my aunt shall name them.

I believe that I am even happier than Jane, for she only smiles. I laugh!

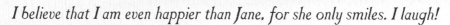

Friday 9th

Oh, I forgot to mention yesterday that Papa has also written a letter – to Mr Collins. This is what he wrote and certainly I couldn't have put it better myself!

Dear Sir,

I must trouble you once more for congratulations. Elizabeth will soon be the wife of Mr Darcy. Console Lady Catherine as well as you can. But, if I were you, I would stand by the nephew. He has more to give. Yours sincerely.

Is it not well said, Lizzy?

I think Papa took much pleasure in writing this letter.

We expect to hear of Mr and Mrs Collins' arrival at the Lucases very shortly. They will have much need to retreat while Lady Catherine's anger dies down! While I will never visit Charlotte again, I will keep up a correspondence with her.

NOVEMBER

Thursday 9th

Dearest Diary,

Just a line to tell you that I am unable to write as my every moment is taken up with wedding plans – such excitement! My dress is to come from Harding and Howell!

I'm all of a spin!

DECEMBER
MY WEDDING DAY ...

This was surely the happiest of days for both Jane and me. I think I might also add the happiest of days for Mr Bingley and my lovely Mr Darcy! The bell of Meryton Church has never pealed so loudly, nor have the streets of Meryton been lined with so many well-wishers!

Saturday 19th

JANE'S TOO!

My excitement was so great that the event really passed in a happy haze, but this is how I imagine it must have been. I do remember that Hill threw lavender confetti in memory of that moment when we first heard that an unattached gentleman was to move into Netherfield!

WEDDING MEMORIES AND TREASURES

The wedding announcement in "The Times". Even Mama thought it well done!

BINGLEY and BENNET, DARCY and BENNET

At Meryton parish church, Mr Bennet, of Longbourn House in Hertfordshire, saw his two elder daughters married; Jane, the eldest, to Mr Charles Bingley, of Netherfield Park in Hertfordshire; and Elizabeth, his second daughter, to Fitzwilliam Darcy, of Pemberley in Derbyshire.

On the morning of our wedding Papa slipped this dear note under my bedroom door.

Dearest Lizzy,

I must admit to making many mistakes as a father, but not with you. You have always given me joy and your wit and perceptions have brought with them many delightful surprises, including your marriage to Mr Darcy!

I shall miss you greatly but, now I am over my initial shock, feel that you have chosen well. It will be a proud father who walks into the local church today with a daughter on each arm. It is as well I have such a fine waistcoat for the occasion!

I look forward to visiting you and your husband at Pemberley – at last a satisfactory reason to venture out of my study and my books!

Bless you, dearest Lizzy.

Your Papa

Mr Bingley and Mr Darcy sent a carriage to take the whole family to Meryton Church. The ponies had flowers and ribbons plaited into their manes. I almost felt in competition with them as they looked so splendid!

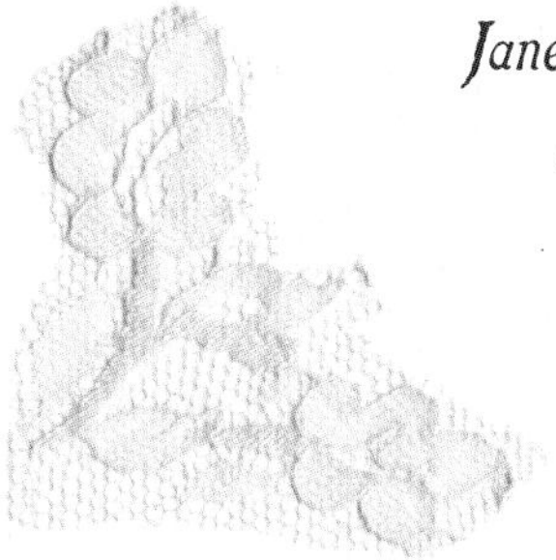

Jane and I did not forget the proverb "Marry in blue, lover be true!" We both wore blue petticoats trimmed with this blue lace. Mr Darcy and Mr Bingley wore blue waistcoats. We will be true, indeed we will.

We chose Psalm 128 as it is so joyful!

My dear Uncle Gardiner played the wheezy old organ for us, while my cousins pumped the bellows! We chose Mozart for our entry and Beethoven for our departure. It was wonderful, but I fear the Minister would have liked a more religious tone.

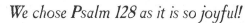

Mama, Cook and Mrs Hill created a lavish wedding breakfast. There was tea, coffee and hot chocolate. Toast, eggs, cold pheasant, game pie, salmon, beef jelly, white soup, raisins and sweets.

My Aunt Philips had iced the wedding cake. It was iced in white and garlanded with pink flowers. She may be an old gossip, but she can ice a cake!

Shortly after the wedding breakfast, Mr and Mrs Bingley and Mr and Mrs Darcy set off in separate coaches to start their new lives together.

It seemed as though the whole of Meryton lined the road to cheer us on our way. As is the tradition, shoes were thrown after us – luckily neither Jane nor I were hit, but both Mr Darcy and Mr Bingley are sporting fine bruises!

Oh, happy, happy day!

PEMBERLEY

Thursday 24th

My dearest Friend,

For that is what you have been this last year or more, I must apologize for neglecting you. You may blame my dear husband, for he takes much getting to know, and being Mrs Fitzwilliam Darcy takes all my time! It is hard to believe that Jane and I were only married a few days ago. We are, without doubt, the happiest of wives.

Now, here I am at Pemberley and I think I shall very soon get used to being its mistress. Mr Darcy is even now downstairs with dear Georgiana, preparing Christmas treats for Mr and Mrs Gardiner and all my lovely cousins. Far from being proud and disagreeable he has already proved to be the most thoughtful and tender of husbands.

I still remember little of our wedding day, except that it was perfect! Papa looked very dashing in his waistcoat and I believe he took great pride in it and his two daughters. He is to visit us for New Year and will bring Kitty, but not Mary or Mama, for they are not good travellers. Jane and Mr Bingley are looking for a property close by and will then quit Netherfield. Imagine my happiness – to have such a husband and my sister just a short distance away.

Lydia writes almost daily, asking me to help her and Wickham. I will do what I can, but I will not mention the matter to Mr Darcy, for there I think I should find his patience with my family at an end. As for Miss Bingley and Lady Catherine, I believe that in the end they will not be able to resist seeing for themselves how Mr Darcy's wife conducts herself. Of course, I shall graciously receive them!

As for me, I think that Lizzy Darcy of Pemberley
will not be writing a novel or even a diary.
I suspect that Lizzy's husband, the most charming and handsome
Mr Fitzwilliam Darcy, will be the keeper of all her secrets
and the one to share in all her joys and sorrows.
And that, my very dear Diary, is just how I wish it to be!

These are Mr Darcy's dogs — I fancy they are quite as characterful as their master!

So, goodbye, dear friend and a very
HAPPY CHRISTMAS AND NEW BEGINNING!
Lizzy Darcy, née Bennet

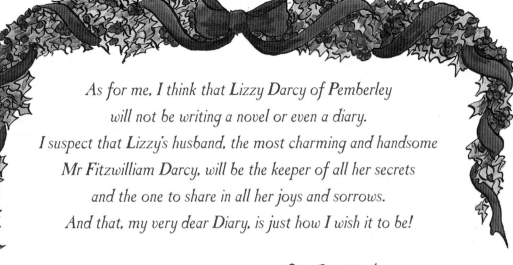

Dear Reader,

I was inspired to create *Lizzy Bennet's Diary* after reading Jane Austen's novel *Pride and Prejudice* for about the tenth time! It has always been one of my favourite books and even though it was published way back in 1813, it still makes me laugh and think about how strange and unpredictable relationships can be. Jane was only twenty-one years old when she wrote the first draft, but I think she already understood a lot about life and love!

Jane Austen

Jane Austen's family had a lot in common with Lizzy Bennet's family, being neither very rich nor very poor. Also, like Lizzy, Jane came from a large family. She was born on 16 December 1775, the second youngest of eight children. She was very close to her brothers and sisters and often read them her stories, and they would put on performances of her plays.

Although she wrote romantic novels, Jane herself never married. She did once accept a marriage proposal, but changed her mind the very next morning! Jane believed that "anything is to be preferred or endured rather than marrying without affection."

Jane's father died suddenly in 1805, and she, her sisters and her mother were left without a place to live: just like the Bennet women, they were barred from inheriting their home. Eventually, Jane's brother Edward invited them to live in a cottage on his Chawton Estate. Jane was happy at Chawton and four of her novels were published while she lived there.

Sadly, in 1816, Jane fell ill and by the spring of 1817 she was confined to bed. Her brother Henry and favourite sister, Cassandra, took her for medical treatment in Winchester, but it was of no help. She died aged forty-one on 18 July 1817.

It wasn't until after her death that Jane Austen's name appeared on her books. Before that the title pages just said "By a Lady". Think how amazed she would be that we are still reading her books today! I hope Jane wouldn't be too cross with me for inventing Lizzy's diary, and I hope you enjoy reading it as much as I have enjoyed creating it.

Marcia Williams

First U.S. edition 2014

Library of Congress Catalog Card Number pending

ISBN 978-0-7636-7030-6

14 15 16 17 18 19 TWP 10 9 8 7 6 5 4 3 2 1

Image credits: page 52: Harding and Howell © The British Library Board (Maps.K.Top.27.20, plate 12); map of London © The British Library Board (Maps Crace Port 6.199); page 70: William Wordsworth © Mary Evans/Epic/PVDE

Printed in Johor Bahru, Malaysia

This book was typeset in Caslon Antique.
The illustrations were done in watercolor, gouache, and ink.

Candlewick Press
99 Dover Street
Somerville, Massachusetts 02144

visit us at
www.candlewick.com

PEMBERLEY DESCRIBED
A personal view by Elizabeth Darcy
Paddocks
Pig pond
North
E W
trees
Stables
Dogs' graves
River Derwent
Footman
Long Drive
Roman garden